TH...
CHARLES WILLIAMS

Also available in Perennial Library by Charles Williams:
DEAD CALM
THE SAILCLOTH SHROUD

THE WRONG VENUS

CHARLES WILLIAMS

HARPER SUSPENSE

PERENNIAL LIBRARY
Harper & Row, Publishers
New York, Cambridge, Philadelphia, San Francisco
London, Mexico City, São Paulo, Sydney

First PERENNIAL LIBRARY edition published 1983.

Library of Congress Cataloging in Publication Data

Williams, Charles, (date)
  The wrong Venus.

  (Perennial library)
  Reprint. Originally published: New York : New
American Library, 1966.
  I. Title.
PS3573.I448W7 1983   813'.54   82-48818
ISBN 0-06-080656-7 (pbk.)

.83 84 85 86 10 9 8 7 6 5 4 3 2 1

Lawrence Colby by the age of thirty had been a Korean paratrooper, art student, PR man, script-writer, a dealer in art forgeries, and newspaperman, and had once ghost-written the autobiography of a homicidal maniac; he had been married twice, once to an Italian actress with kleptomania and once to a wealthy middle-aged woman who stoned embassies and slugged cops with protest signs at demonstrations; he had been beaten up in riots, shot through the leg in Houston, Texas, by a woman who was trying to kill her husband, and had been down the Cresta Run at St. Moritz three times; but afterward he was prone to look back on all this part of his life before he met Martine Randall as a time when nothing ever happened.

They met just a week after his thirtieth birthday, on a flight from Geneva to London. . . .

The flight had already been announced when he checked in **at** Cointrin, so he was the last passenger to board. There were two aisle seats left in the first-class section, one beside a bearded two-hundred-pound Sikh in travel-soiled khaki and the other next to a dream of a girl who was reading the European edition of *Time*, a luscious brunette with a striking figure and deep blue eyes. She glanced up briefly as he came to a decision and sat down.

"I beg your pardon," he said, after he had fastened his seat belt and verified his first appraisal of the legs, "but aren't you Pamela McCarthy?"

She smiled shyly. "Not really, I'm afraid. Pamela's my roommate. I just borrowed her leg." She went back to the *Time*.

He sighed. "Well, I'll tell her you're taking good care of it. . . . Goodnight, David." Lowering his seat back, he closed his eyes.

Normally, he would have probed the defenses at least once more, as the minimal tribute to so much girl, but he was tired:

1

he'd been up most of the night before. In a minute or two he had dozed off, and was only vaguely aware when the plane taxied to the runway and made its take-off run. He was awakened briefly by a stewardess offering lunch, but waved it off, and went back to sleep again.

Then he was dreaming he was riding a roller coaster in an amusement park, a ride full of vertiginous swoops and sudden upswings that threatened to throw him out of the car. It seemed to go on forever. When he awoke at last he saw that the plane had run into turbulence. White wool streaked past outside the windows, and the FASTEN SEAT BELTS sign was on.

They dropped a hundred feet in a sickening lunge that threw him up against his belt, then fishtailed, yawing wildly. He glanced at his watch and saw they should be down in London in less than an hour. Apparently the turbulence had been going on for some time. Most of the other passengers had dozed off, but up forward he could hear somebody being sick. A stewardess came down the aisle clinging to the seats with one hand and carrying one of the white bags in the other.

The plane shot upward and to port. The stewardess grabbed for the back of Colby's seat, missed, and caught his shoulder. She smiled. "So soddy." She was very British.

Colby grinned up at her and winked with the kinship of those immune to motion sickness. He turned to look at the girl beside him. She had put her seat back so it was level with his, and was apparently asleep, her face near his shoulder. She was probably in her late twenties, but there was an almost childlike innocence about her face in repose. It was a fine-boned face with a good chin and a beautiful clear complexion, the lashes dark smudges against her skin. Her lips were slightly parted, and he was conscious of the impulse to kiss her. That was just what he needed, he thought, to go through Customs at London with his face under his left ear. The plane bucketed up and down, and took a long skidding dive to starboard.

He had just turned away and was reaching for a cigarette when he thought he heard her say something. He hoped she wasn't going to be sick. Colby genuinely liked women, and never

2

felt any resentment at having been given the brush; if they didn't knock down the proffered arm of fellowship a good part of the time, by now there wouldn't be room left to stand.

He looked around at her. "I beg your pardon?"

Her eyes were still closed, but her lips moved. "You're ticking."

He frowned. "I'm what?"

The lips moved again, the words just faintly audible. "You're ticking."

He felt the first intimation of horror. The plane bounced upward, yawed, and plummeted again.

The damned turbulence! And it hadn't even occurred to him till now. . . . While he was still numb with this first chill of realization, she spoke again from beside his shoulder, the words inaudible to anyone else. "I hope you're not carrying a bomb?"

Maybe he could convince her she'd only imagined the ticking. "Well, actually, it's just an old prewar model. They don't go off half the time."

He stopped. The lips had begun to curve upward at the corners; the eyes opened, and for the first time he saw into them, saw the laughter, the blazing intelligence, and the devil. She knew damned well what he was carrying.

"They're self-winding?" she asked.

He nodded dumbly, trying to think of something. He listened, but he still couldn't hear them. Probably only a few had started now, but her ear was nearer them, or her hearing was better. Of course, it was impossible to hear the ticking of a watch more than a few inches away, especially over the rushing sound of the plane's ventilating system, but fifty of them ticking together was something else. And when they all started—good God!

"How many?" she whispered.

"Three hundred."

Then, just as he remembered with horror that a hundred of them were alarms, with either buzzers or chimes, there was a faint musical tinkle from inside his sweater. It repeated itself twice, very slowly, before it ran down.

He shuddered and looked around at the girl. Her hand was

3

up to her mouth, and the eyes were overflowing with silent blue laughter. He wanted to strangle her.

"I'm sorry," she gasped. "I was just thinking of you going through Customs sounding like the 'Bell Song' from *Lakmé*——"

The plane bounced, lurched from side to side, and swooped again. He closed his eyes and could see the three hundred little rotors swinging, storing energy. Damn the Swiss and their ingenuity.

"——and on a flight from Geneva," the girl went on in that faint voice full of suppressed mirth. "But I'll come visit you at Wormwood Scrubs. . . . Or I'm sure Pamela will."

"If I had your sense of humor," Colby said, "I'd never fly. I'd just hang around airports waiting for somebody to crash."

"Oh, don't be silly. We'll get you through Customs some way."

"We?"

"Of course." She gestured impatiently. "It was just that you sound so funny, ticking away like a big tweed bomb."

There was another silvery tinkle from inside Colby's sweater. *Ding . . . ding . . . ding . . . ding. . . .*

"It must be four p.m. in New Delhi," she said, mirth bubbling up in the eyes again.

"Look——" Colby snapped.

"Precisely." The teasing devils disappeared from her eyes, and they narrowed with thought. "That's the first thing." She gestured significantly toward the seats in front and back of them.

Colby unsnapped his belt and stood up, pretending to search for something in the overhead rack. He had to grab the edge of the rack to remain upright as the plane dropped away from under him, hit an ascending column of air, and bounced upward again. He looked around.

The two passengers in front of him, obviously businessmen, were discussing something in German. They could probably understand English, but were busy with their own affairs. In the seats directly behind, a woman was being sick into a bag while the young boy beside her read one of the *Tintin* books, French, or French-Swiss. The boy wouldn't know English yet, and if the woman did she was too sick to care if they blew up the plane.

4

Directly across from them, the Sikh was asleep, his beard a cresting hirsute wave poised above his chest.

Nobody was astir in the aisle except the two stewardesses going back and forth with Dramamine or carrying away the paper bags of those who hadn't taken it soon enough. He sat down, strapped himself in, and turned, his face close to hers. He could feel time rushing by him like the shredded tufts of vapor flung backward past the windows. He had to think of something, and damned fast.

"Even if the turbulence stopped now," he said, "they won't run down before we land at London."

She glanced at her watch. "It's less than forty minutes. We've got to stop them some way."

"If we had a magnet——" He stopped. Where would you find a magnet aboard a plane? And the damned things were probably anti-magnetic anyway. Trust the Swiss.

"How are you carrying them?" she asked.

Colby was dressed in a shapeless old tweed suit and light-weight green sweater. Under his shirt was a vestlike garment made up of three hundred individual pockets. He told her.

"They're just movements?" she asked.

"Of course." Nobody ever smuggled watches in cases.

"Then just go into the loo, take off the vest thing, and dunk it in the washbasin."

"It's not that simple. Each one's sealed in a little plastic bag."

"Oh." She looked thoughtful. "I'm not sure water would do it, anyway. They might start again. . . . Something viscous— I've got it!" The blue eyes lighted up, and she pushed the button for the stewardess.

"What?" Colby asked.

"A liqueur of some kind. Cointreau—crème de menthe——"

"Hey, sure!"

The stewardess came. It was the tall dark one. Just as she leaned in over Colby, holding onto the seat in front, there was a faint *ding . . . ding . . .* from inside his sweater. He jerked his left arm in across his chest, shook the wrist, and looked at the watch with annoyance.

5

The stewardess held out an empty airsickness bag, automatically searching the floor for the other one. Colby waved off the bag. "Do you have any Cointreau?"

"Cointreau?" It was obvious she thought he was crazy.

"You do sell liquor on these flights, don't you?"

"Yes, of course. . . . But with this turbulence, naturally we couldn't bring the cart through. And we don't have any Cointreau, anyway."

"Then crème de menthe?"

"Y-e-e-s, I think so. But I'm afraid only the white——"

He was conscious again of time hurtling past him, but managed a reassuring smile. "It's all right. I only drink in the dark."

She went away and came back in a minute with the bottle. He paid her. She departed, holding onto the seats.

"After you get stripped down to that vest," the girl whispered, "unlock the door. I'll come in and help you."

"You might get caught."

"I'll pick a time when they're not looking. Don't argue, you'll never get them done alone."

"Right. And thanks a lot."

"Hurry."

He unsnapped his belt and stowed the bottle in a pocket of his jacket. Both stewardesses were busy forward. The washroom was three rows back, on the starboard side. He made it, having to stop and hang onto the seats only once.

It was the usual small compartment, not much more than four feet square, with the chemical toilet in one corner and a small washbasin and mirror on the forward wall. He bolted the door, set the bottle in the basin, and began hurriedly throwing off his upper clothing, hanging the tweed jacket, sweater, shirt, and tie on the hook on the back of the door. For a moment, miraculously, the plane was steady. Just as he was down to the vest at last, one of the buzzer alarms went off with a raucous vitality that sent a shiver up his back. They were putting on muscle by the minute.

He stabbed at one of the pockets at random, and saw it was going to be impossible to get the watches out while still wearing the vest; the fabric was too tight, and the tiny slits too narrow to put his fingers into. He unzipped it and set it beside the basin, nude to the waist now. Just as he picked up the bottle of crème de menthe to unscrew the cap, he remembered the door. He unbolted it. Almost at the same instant, it swung open, and the girl slipped inside. She closed and locked it. Colby tossed the bottle aside.

"Just pour it in the basin," she said, "and we'll dip them in it—oops——!"

The plane lurched sidewise. They wound up in the corner beside the door. She was behind him, one arm around his waist and her chin propped on his shoulder. Colby still held onto the bottle, outthrust and aloft but upright.

"Cozy, isn't it?" she asked.

The plane lurched again, to the left this time, and they shot off the door toward the opposite wall. Colby put out a hand and stopped them before they slammed into it. They managed to untangle themselves. The plane steadied. He closed the wash-basin drain and upended the bottle over it. It gurgled. She had already reached for the vest, and was sliding watch movements from the bottom row of pockets.

He stowed the empty bottle in the used-towel disposal. She had two of the watch movements out now and was trying to break open one of the little plastic bags in which they were sealed. It was tough, and she was making slow work of it. She solved this by taking a corner of it between her teeth and tearing it. He tore the other open. Together they dipped the two of them into the crème de menthe. The malevolent pulsing of the mainsprings died with the first contact, like spiders in cyanide. They looked at each other and winked. Then the plane dropped from under them.

They were against the door in a frozen and exaggerated tango step, the girl leaning backward under him with her face against his chest, looking upward. His clothing, which had flown off the hook, began to settle. The shirt fell across his head like a white burnoose. She grinned, and began to hum "The Sheik of Araby."

The plane was shooting upward now and he couldn't straighten against the pull of gravity. Something was digging into his

7

shoulder, and he realized that it was the watch movement she still had in her hand. He looked around on the floor for the other.

"It's in my bra," she said.

"Oh . . . which side?"

"Don't be so technical."

The plane's upward lunge ceased abruptly and it lurched to port. Colby swung up off the door like an inverted pendulum and staggered back in another tango step with the girl still in his arms. He sat down on the chemical toilet, which fortunately was closed, and she came over onto him, clutching his head with his face pressed into her breast.

"I can feel it," he said.

"*You* can feel it? I can tell what time it stopped."

They flew upright again. This time Colby managed to execute a turn step before they were plastered against the door once more, so his back was against it.

She pulled her face out of his shoulder and turned it up to look at him. "If you have a free hand, would you see if you can pull my skirt down?"

Colby reached down and tugged, but it was caught between them. "I'm sorry. Maybe on the next step across. . . ."

"Well, I suppose at least we could introduce ourselves. I'm Martine Randall."

"How do you do? My name's Lawrence Colby."

"I'm sorry about the lipstick on your chest."

"That's all right——" The plane topped out and yawed again. They took a step off the door and then back against it. "Is your skirt all right now?" he asked.

"I think so. I don't feel tweed any more."

"Is it Mrs. Randall, or Miss Randall?"

"I'm divorced."

"So am I."

The plane was on an even keel for a few seconds. She removed one arm from around his neck and shoved her hand down between them. When it emerged she was holding the watch movement. She glanced at it. "Ten till eleven," she said. "I'll probably look like a stamped timecard the rest of my life."

One of the watches began to buzz in the vest, which was lying on the floor under the washbasin. Colby glanced at his own watch and felt the chill along his nerves again. They were due in London in twenty-five minutes, and so far they'd stopped two of them.

But maybe they were out of the turbulence. The plane continued to bore straight ahead. They untangled themselves and he grabbed up the vest. In a moment they had evolved a system. She pushed them out of the pockets, Colby bit off the plastic bag, dropped the latter in the towel disposal, dipped the watch movement in the crème de menthe, handed it back to her, and she returned it to the vest. They worked swiftly and in silence. He counted . . . ten . . . thirty . . . forty-five . . . sixty. . . .

Twenty minutes to London.

The plane slammed into another wall of turbulence. It shot ρward and to the right, and they were against the door again. "Damn!" Colby said.

"And just when we were doing so beautifully——"

The knob rattled, and on the other side of the door a feminine voice called out, "I'm sorry, but I must ask you to return to your seats——" There was a horrified gasp, and then the voice went on, "You can't be in there *together*!"

"Why not?" Colby asked. "It doesn't say so."

"Of course not, but everybody *knows*——"

That was just what they needed, he thought—a refresher course in *la différence* while the plane continued to zero in on London at four hundred miles an hour. Why the hell did she have to be passing the john at that particular moment?

The knob rattled again. "Open the door immediately, or I shall have to call the First Officer!"

The plane steadied for a moment. "I'll get rid of her," Martine whispered in his ear. Snatching up the vest, she shoved it in his hand and motioned for him to drop it behind the chemical toilet. As he straightened and turned, facing her and the door again, she winked, opened her mouth wide, and put her hand on her stomach with a grimace of pain. Then she reached around in back and unlatched the door, which flew open. It was the short,

9

red-haired stewardess, the one who looked Scottish, bristling with Presbyterian outrage. Colby opened his mouth and groaned. It was happening a little fast for him, but that seemed to be what she'd meant.

The stewardess gasped again, staring at his naked chest, or as much of it as was visible past Martine Randall. *"Well!"*

"Wider," Martine ordered, peering intently into the back of his mouth. Colby repeated the groan, with his hand pressed to his lower abdomen. He hoped this was where the pain was supposed to be. She tilted his head a little, as though for better light. "Strange . . . very strange. . . ."

"Really!"

". . . certainly no evidence of Barker's syndrome," Martine went on. Then, as though aware of the stewardess for the first time, she snapped, "Yes, yes, what is it? Must you stand there yammering?"

"This gentleman *cannot* be in here with his clothes off!"

Martine turned with a withering glance. "Do you expect him to take them off out in the cabin? Don't just stand there, bring me an electric torch and a spoon."

"What—? What for?"

Martine sighed. "My dear girl, I asked for a torch and a spoon on the assumption that you do *not* have a laryngoscope aboard your aircraft. In the event that I have underestimated its facilities, please accept my apologies, and bring the laryngoscope instead. And quickly——"

The stewardess began to look uncertain. "You're a physician?"

"Bravo, that's a good girl. . . . Smartly, now——"

"But what's wrong with him? He looks all right."

"My dear, I'm sure the airline wouldn't want to add the burden of medical diagnosis to your other——"

The plane lurched. The stewardess shot inward and the door slammed shut behind her. Colby was against the outer wall, now with two girls suspended from his neck. Somewhere under him, in the vest hidden behind the toilet, a watch buzzed its rattle-snake warning, and the stewardess spoke with Britannic firmness into his throat. "Really, I must insist that you return to your seats." There would always be an England, Colby thought. Not to mention Switzerland.

The plane shot upward. Martine peeled off and sat down on the toilet seat. Colby and his new partner came over against the door, and then upright again. The door flew open. It was the Frenchwoman from the seat behind them. She took in Colby's naked shoulders and the stewardess clasped in his arms. Her eyes rolled to heaven. "*Alors . . . les anglais!*"

The Sikh appeared in the passageway behind her. Oh, no, Colby thought, not two more! "*Ne restez pas——*" he began, when the plane staggered to port and the door scooped them in. It was like a valve, he thought, or the entrance to a lobster pot. His face was full of beard now like a burst carton of shredded wheat, and upward through this foliage came cries of, "*Lâchez-moi! Lâchez-moi!*" and another fateful buzzing from the vest. He closed his eyes. There was no longer any hope.

The plane lurched, but there was no danger now of being thrown from side to side; they were too tightly wedged.

"*Lâchez-moi! Ouvrez la porte, espèce de chameau——!*"

"*Ouvrez-la vous-même,*" Colby said. "*Vous êtes plus près.*"

The Sikh had somehow taken a phrase book from the breast pocket of his jacket and was holding it over his head. "*Pouvez-vous me dire,*" he asked, "*où se trouve le cabinet de toilette?*"

"Just follow the crowds," Colby said into the beard. "You can't miss it."

"Oh, you are English."

"American. . . . Can anybody reach the doorknob?"

"*Au secours! Au secours!*"

"Really, you must return to your seats——"

Bzzzzzzzzzzzzzzzzzzz——!

"I can feel it," the Sikh replied. "It is in the middle of my back. . . . It is urgent that I find the W.C."

"Well, hang on, for Christ's sake. . . . Try to reach the knob——"

"I cannot——"

"You cannot reach the knob, or you cannot hang on?"

"To the rescue!" It was the Frenchwoman; she must have a phrase book of her own. "I am menaced by English ravishers."

"He certainly is *not* English," the stewardess disclaimed, speaking into the other side of his throat. "He's an American."

"*Comment?*"

"*Il n'est pas anglais——*"

It would be a great place for Berlitz to open a branch, Colby thought, if they could squeeze in. He could feel Martine behind him, pulling herself up along his right arm. "Can't anybody reach the door?" he pleaded.

She was erect behind him now, leaning on his shoulder. "I'm going to try," she said.

"*Quoi encore?*" demanded the Frenchwoman, hearing this new voice. "*Y a-t-il une autre femme? D'où vient-elle?*"

"She was sitting on the toilet," the stewardess explained. "Excuse me—I mean, *elle était assise*——"

"*Alors . . . les anglais!*"

"It's all right," Martine reassured the stewardess. "Don't back down an inch. I'm American, too."

Even in all this madness, Colby was conscious of surprise. He'd thought she was English. He felt her lips against his ear, and she whispered, "Don't put it back on. I've got another idea."

"So have I," he said. "Ditch it." Losing all that money was better than going to prison.

"No. . . . But bring it out under your jacket."

"If I ever get the jacket on again."

"I think I can make it to the door, across the top." Her voice came from above him now, and he realized that she had stepped up on the toilet. "If the two of you will hold me."

"It is of the utmost urgency——" the Sikh began.

"Hang on! Hang on!" Colby said. "The cavalry's coming." He gestured upward and behind him. "Pass her across, and she'll reach down behind you and turn the knob."

Her weight was on his shoulder. He caught her under the arms and pushed up and outward until she was lying in a more or less horizontal plane across the top of the compartment above them.

"Almost there——" she gasped.

"*J'ai l'impression qu'il y a encore une autre femme, au plafond,*" the Frenchwoman remarked in a tone that denoted only mild wonder. The English were losing their ability to surprise her.

"On the ceiling?" the stewardess asked, somewhere under the beard. "Really, she *must* return to her seat."

"I've got the knob," Martine said. At the same moment, the door swung open and she was face to face with the First Officer, at a distance of some four inches. She smiled. "Oh, hello. . . ."

The latter paled, apparently having never opened a door on anything quite like it. Then, during that brief rupture of the

13

thought process when the rational mind refuses to ingest the manifestly impossible, automatic good manners rushed in to fill the breach. "I *am* sorry."

"It's all right," Martine said. "I was just coming out."

This time the plane yawed to starboard. They all came out.

There was another rap on the door. "Really, you must hurry."

The plane banked. They were already commencing their approach. Colby fastened the collar and one other button of his shirt, knotted the tie, and yanked the sweater on over his head. He put on the tweed jacket, and reached down behind the chemical toilet for the vest. He could hear the ticking itself now; all the remaining two hundred and forty were brimming with poisonous vitality and chewing their way into oncoming generations of time like an army of steel-mandibled termites. Great! Just great. Send for our Little Gem Watch-Smuggler's Kit, and get into this big-paying field at once. Be the first in your neighborhood with prison pallor.

The plane turned again, and continued to lose altitude in their inexorable approach to the runways at London Airport and Her Majesty's Customs officers. He had an impression of being poured down through some great funnel into a jug labeled Wormwood Scrubs, with no way to turn aside, or go back, or even to stop or slow down. He shoved the vest up inside the jacket, clamped it with an arm, and buttoned the jacket. As far as he could tell, it didn't show.

He hurried out. Just as he started up the aisle, the plane went into another steep bank, and he had to cling to the back of a seat, conscious of all the furious activity against his ribs. With only ten minutes more, they'd have had it made.

The man in the seat glanced up. "I say, you don't happen to have the time?" He gave an apologetic little smile. "My watch appears to have stopped."

Colby stared down at him wordlessly, held out his watch so the man could see it, and lunged forward to his seat. His topcoat was lying in it. He grabbed it up, sat down, and fastened his belt. The plane was already dropping toward the end of the runway.

He leaned toward Martine, and whispered, "I'd better leave 'em. Ditch 'em under a seat——"

"Don't be silly. I said I'd get you through Customs, didn't I?" She was smiling, her eyes bright with excitement. "We'll muffle them, to start with. Roll the vest in your topcoat, and then in this." He noticed then that she had a fur coat across her lap. Apparently the stewardess had just returned it to her.

The plane touched down, bounced once, and began to decelerate. There was nobody in the aisle yet, and across from them the Sikh was looking out the window. Colby pulled the vest out, rolled it in the gabardine topcoat, and then in the fur, which he noted was natural mink. He wondered why she was doing it.

"Good," she said. "Now, here's the drill. Do you have a bag aboard the plane?"

"Yes."

"No contraband in it?" Mirth welled up in the eyes again like bubbles in champagne. "No atom-bomb assemblies, dirty pictures, hashish . . . ?"

"No," he replied.

"All right. Give me the check. I'll claim it, along with mine, and you won't have to get close to the Customs counter at all. You just carry the coats for us. Is there any chance they know you and may be watching for you?"

"No," he said. "This is the first time."

"Good. . . . The only two places that'll be a little tricky will be going through passport control and past the guard at the exit from Customs." She grinned, and held out a hand. "Good luck."

"Thanks a million. . . . But why are you doing it?"

The excitement showed in her eyes again. "I wouldn't have missed it for anything."

The plane came to rest. The engines died, and with them the rushing sound of the ventilating system. In the sudden silence, Colby held the bundled coats up across his chest, inclined his head, and listened. The ticking was well muffled, and sounded faint and far away. Their eyes met, and he was on the point of winking when one of the alarms went off with a buzz that would have been audible for ten feet. Sweat broke out on his face. Pas-

15

sengers were already pouring out into the aisle and going past them. There was no possibility of unwrapping the bundle now and disposing of the watches without being seen.

"Relax," Martine said out of the corner of her mouth. "We can always create a diversion."

He stepped out into the aisle, feeling the sides of the funnel close in around him again. Just in front of them was the Frenchwoman, laden with a fur coat and an armful of packages. As they passed the washroom, she tapped on the door, and said, *"Dépêche-toi, mon chéri."*

The boy emerged, the one who'd been reading the *Tintin* book. He was plucking at shreds of paper towel that appeared to be stuck to his fingers.

"England is a crazy country," he said in French. "The water's sticky, and smells like peppermint."

"Quoi encore?" The Frenchwoman snatched at his hand and sniffed. *"Alors . . . les anglais!"*

Colby sighed. He'd forgotten to drain the crème de menthe from the basin, but it didn't matter anyway. He'd either make it through the gauntlet ahead or he wouldn't. They came down the ramp and started toward the entrance to the terminal building. There was still silence from inside the coats. The woman handed the boy one of the things she'd been carrying; Martine and Colby saw and recognized it at the same instant. It was a transistor radio. They looked at each other.

Colby turned to the boy with a beaming smile. *"Connais-tu les Beatles?"* He did a couple of bodily contortions he hoped approximated the writhings of Beatle fans, and snapped out a lively, "Yeah . . . yeah!"

"Attention! C'est le fou!" the Frenchwoman warned, apparently on the point of clutching her son to her and running for police protection, but the seed had been planted. The boy had already switched on the radio and was turning the dial. The first station was a BBC program.

". . . of course, this is merely one of the many ecological factors to be considered in any study of the distribution patterns of the bearded titmouse. . . ."

Sensing that this might not take him by the throat, Colby was on the point of springing forward to help him find something else when the boy turned the dial again and the radio erupted with guitar and voice.

"Ah!" Colby sighed with ecstasy and turned to Martine. "The Beatles!"

The boy looked at him with contempt. "Johnny Hallyday."

"*J'aime Johnny Hallyday,*" Colby said.

They were inside the terminal now, in the long line stretching up to the passport counter, Martine first, then Colby, the boy with his blaring radio, and his mother. More passengers entered the line behind them. They moved slowly ahead.

One of the watches chimed inside the coats—*ding . . . ding . . . ding*—but the sound was lost and all but inaudible under that from the radio. Colby turned and smiled at the boy, and beat time to the music with his hand.

Come on, Johnny, he prayed, keep laying it in there, kid.

Only ten now between them and the desk. Eight. The song cut off, and there was a short announcement in French. Colby held his breath. Music blared again. He sighed. Five more to go . . . four . . . two. . . .

Martine was tendering her passport to the man in the window. Colby had his out and ready. The music stopped, and a voice was speaking French. Colby, his nerves pulled tight, and only half listening to it, was vaguely aware it was a report on food prices at Les Halles.

Whack! Martine's passport was stamped and handed back to her. Colby passed his in. He was squarely in front of the officer now.

". . . *entrecôte vingt-deux francs le kilo.* . . ."

One of the watches began to chime—*ding . . . ding.* . . . "Zut!" the boy said, and clicked off the radio. *Ding!* In the sudden and horrifying silence, it sounded like Big Ben.

"No—wait!" Colby whirled, plucked the radio from him, and snapped on the switch. The officer looked up curiously from his routine glance at the passport photograph. The radio came on, blaring. "This could be it!" Colby snapped.

17

". . . *haricots verts un franc dix le kilo, aubergine deux francs vingt le kilo* . . ."

He listened, eyes narrowed, tense, modern man living in the shadow of the Bomb. "Everything could depend on this——!"

"On the price of eggplant?" the officer asked.

So they had to get one that spoke French. "I'm in the produce business," he said.

"Odd. . . . Your passport says you're a writer."

"That's right. I cover the European produce markets for the *Wall Street Journal.*"

"Oh." The officer shrugged and reached for his stamp. Always joking, these chaps. The watch stopped chiming. Colby sighed.

"*Rendez la moi!*" The boy grabbed the radio, turned it off, and kicked him in the shin. "*Salaud!*"

Whack! The officer stamped Colby's passport and was handing it back.

One of the alarms cut loose. *Bzzzzzzzzz!*

"Darling!" Martine shrieked. "The Westrays! Over there!" She clutched his arm and waved toward the crowds beyond the barrier.

"Where?" Colby whirled, waved a frantic greeting, and roared, "Bill! You old sidewinder, you old polecat——!"

"Marge! . . . Yoo-hoo, Marge, darling——!"

He had the passport now, and they were hurrying on, still shouting.

"*Alors . . . les anglais!*"

"*Américains, madame,*" the officer said.

In Customs, Colby stood well back on rubbery legs while she claimed the bags, told the officer there was nothing in them to declare, and that she'd brought in no gifts. She called a porter and turned them over to him.

There remained only the guard at the door. She grinned at Colby. "Let's go."

They started out. When they were ten feet short of the doorway, too late to turn back without looking suspicious, one of the

18

watches began to chime and another went off with a strident buzz, but she was between him and the guard, shouting:

"I DON'T KNOW WHY YOU BOUGHT THE STUPID HEARING AID IN THE FIRST PLACE IF YOU'RE NOT GOING TO WEAR IT! DON'T BE SUCH AN IDIOT! LOTS OF YOUNG MEN ARE DEAF! YOU MIGHT AS WELL HAVE THROWN THE THREE HUNDRED DOLLARS DOWN A WELL FOR ALL THE GOOD IT DOES YOU——!"

They were past.

His right eardrum might be permanently paralyzed, but they'd made it. He went on out of earshot of the guard and collapsed against a wall. With trembling fingers he lighted a cigarette, and when he looked around she was laughing. He began to laugh too.

"I'll never be able to thank you," he said.

"Forget it. It was fun."

"I'm taking a taxi into town. Could I give you a lift?"

"Thanks awfully, but somebody's meeting me."

"Well, how about dinner tonight?"

"I wish I could," she replied. "But I have some business to attend to——"

"Martine! Martine!"

They looked around. A man was hurrying toward them through the crowd, a tall, rail-thin man apparently in a state of great agitation. He was bareheaded, but wore a light topcoat which flapped out behind him.

"Oh-oh. Your problem was nothing." Martine took her coat from Colby. "Good luck." She started toward the man, but paused. "Where are you staying in London?"

"The Green Park Hotel," he replied.

She nodded, waved goodbye, and turned to greet the other. Colby stood watching them, sorry to see her go.

"Thank God you got here," the man said. He took her hand, shook it once, and dropped it as though it were something he'd grabbed up by mistake on his way out of a burning building. "I've got to get back to Paris. She still hasn't shown up——"

"All right, all right, Merriman, calm down," Martine soothed. He would be named Merriman, Colby thought; he looked as if he had a backlog of ulcers waiting for locations. They disappeared

19

into the crowd, the man still gesturing violently. ". . . fifty pages to go. Writers! I'd rather be in hell with a broken back. . . ."

Colby reclaimed his bag from the porter and found a taxi. He delivered the watches to an oily-looking importer in the back room of an office in Soho, and explained the gummy condition of sixty of them.

"Whose stupid idea was that?" the importer complained. "Now I'll have to have them cleaned."

Colby hit him. He extracted his pay from the man's wallet, thoughtfully regarded the empty vest, dropped it in his face, and went out. He saw the evening performance of *A Funny Thing Happened on the Way to the Forum*, and had dinner afterward at Cunningham's, still thinking dazedly of Martine Randall.

She was without doubt the most disturbing, provocative, and beautiful girl he'd ever run into, and anybody who could come up that naturally and easily with an idea like pouring crème de menthe in watch movements while being thrown around in a storm twenty thousand feet over France was endowed with no plodding, pedestrian mind. But who was she? She had an American passport, but her speech was English—at least part of the time—while the name Martine was French. Well, he'd never know; like an idiot he hadn't even asked her address. When he got back to the hotel at eleven P.M. there were two telephone messages from her. Would he call her at the Savoy Hotel? His heart leaped. Would he!

Her extension was busy. He tried seven times in the next forty-five minutes, and finally got through to her just before midnight. She sounded glad to hear him, but rushed.

"Are you by any chance looking for a job?" she asked.

Nothing had been further from his thoughts. "Sure," he said eagerly. "What is it?"

"It's a little unusual, and I can't explain now," she replied. "I'm waiting for a call from Paris. But would you come to my room here at nine in the morning?"

"I could come right now," he offered. "You know how it is when you're out of work, the anxiety, the insecurity——"

"Oh, I'm sure you'll survive the night, Mr. Colby." She hung up.

It was ten minutes till nine when he knocked on her door at the Savoy next morning. She opened it and smiled a greeting. She seemed to be wearing practically nothing, and was eating a herring.

I t was one of those mornings Colby loved best in London—
that rare October day when miraculously it was cursed with
neither the Automobile Show nor rain. Pale lemon sunlight
slanted in on the carpet at the other end of the room where her
window overlooked the traffic on the Thames. A breakfast cart
draped with a white cloth was parked near an armchair, on it a
silver coffee pot and a covered chafing dish.

"Please sit down," she said, indicating another armchair near
the writing desk. The dark hair was rumpled, and she wore no
make-up except a touch of lipstick. Her uniform of the day, at
least up to this point, seemed to consist of nylon briefs, bra, a
sheer peignoir that wasn't even very carefully belted, and one
fur-trimmed mule. In her left hand was a plate containing the
herring, or what was left of it. She sat down crosswise in the armchair with a flash of long bare legs, kicked off the other mule,
and stretched like a cat. She grinned at Colby. "A little stiff after
that workout yesterday. How about a kipper?"

"No, thanks," he said.

"Coffee?"

"Thanks, I just had breakfast."

"I love 'em," she said. "Kippers, I mean. Every time I'm in
London, I go on a regular orgy."

"You went to school in England, didn't you?" he asked. In his
opinion it was a taste that had to be acquired young, when resistance to any kind of food was minimal and rebellion ineffectual.

"Yes, for a time. But to get to the matter of the job I mentioned
—you're a writer, I understand."

"I have been," he replied. "Among other things."

"What kind of writing have you done? I mean, when you're
not covering the world eggplant situation?"

"Newspaper work, mostly police beat. A few PR jobs. And a little script-writing in Paris."

She nodded, seeming lost in thought, and lifted the cover off the chafing dish. "You're sure you won't have a kipper?"

"No, thanks." He took out a cigarette.

She forked another herring onto her plate and attacked it with relish. "How are you at sex?"

"I was hoping you would ask that," Colby said. "When you finish your herring——"

"No, I mean, how are you at writing about it?"

"I don't know. I never tried."

"That's probably the reason you're smuggling watches for a living. You're out of the mainstream of contemporary thought."

"I suppose so," he agreed. "It just never seemed to me it got anywhere on paper. Too much like trying to barbecue a rainbow."

"Of course. But you're missing the point."

"Just what is the job?"

"A friend of mine is trying to get a novel written, a bedroom western——"

"Why?" he asked. "Trying to find something to read on a newsstand now, you're up to your earlobes in melon-heavy breasts."

"The market's assured." She whistled softly. "And *what* a market. You've heard of Sabine Manning, of course?"

"Sure, who hasn't?"

"You have to take the pills just to read her stuff. Anyway, this friend of mine, a man named Merriman Dudley——"

"The one that met you at the airport yesterday?"

"That's right. He's her business agent, handles her money, investments, and so on. Well, he's in something of a jam, and since in a way it was my fault, I've been trying to help him out."

"Mrs. Manning lives here in London?"

"She has a house here—or did, rather—and another in Paris. But I'd better clue you in and scrape off a little of the PR job. It's not Mrs. Manning. It's Miss Manning. And that's a pen name."

Fleurelle Scudder, to use her real name, had been a government clerk in Washington, in a minor department of a bureau set up to purchase cavalry ponchos during the Spanish-American

War and then lost in some organizational reshuffle, to live on into the space age with that eerie viability characteristic of government agencies. She'd started working for the bureau during World War II, and typed away in there for years, among the cobwebs and yellowing memoranda from Colonel Roosevelt, going home at night to her room at the Y.W.C.A. So she wrote a novel.

"Something-or-other *In the Flesh*," Colby said.

"*Violence in the Flesh*. Did you read it?"

"Only the jacket blurbs. I wasn't quite twenty-three then, and I was afraid I wasn't ready for it. In the army, and knocking around Paris, you lead a pretty sheltered life compared to an American suburb."

It sold two hundred thousand in hard cover, and into the millions in paperback. Then there was the motion picture, of course, which had the good fortune to be denounced by more religious and civic groups than any other film in a decade. She was thirty-six when *Violence* came out, and in the past seven years she'd turned out four more for a take of somewhere around a million and a half. Then Martine derailed the gravy train—unintentionally, of course. She sold her a painting.

"Must have been pretty hairy," Colby said. "Pop, or op?"

"No, it wasn't the painting itself, but a question of ownership." She dug at the kipper, smiled, and went on. "At the time I was divorced from my husband there was a bit of a *bagarre* over the community property—you know the type of thing, with battalions of lawyers charging back and forth over the same terrain for weeks on end—so being a little short of cash at the moment I took custody of the art collection, two Picassos, a Dufy, and a Braque."

It hadn't seemed to her an exorbitant return for three years of boredom, but Old Ironpants—her husband's mother—had come charging in from Florence like a wounded rhino and begun putting lawyers up trees all over the field. Martine's lawyer had pointed out that due to some legal nonsense about her having already quit the conjugal bed plus the fact that she had removed the paintings at two o'clock in the morning with the help of a professional burglar, she was in something of an untenable position and she'd better give them back. The trouble was, she'd already sold one of them. The Braque. To Sabine Manning.

"Of course, that was Old Ironpants' favorite, and she told the lawyers the Braque would be returned or she'd have three inches off the top of my skull for a birdbath. Personally, I thought it was a big flap about nothing. I'd always believed the Braque was a forgery."

Something nudged at Colby's mind. Mother and son? "What was your husband's name?"

"Jonathan Courtney Sisson," she said. "The Fourth."

He nodded. "It was a fake. I sold it to him."

"I thought so. Anyway, I had to get it back, and I'd already spent the money. So the only thing to do was make a copy of it and return the copy."

Fortunately, the painting was in Miss Manning's London house, and she was in Paris. Dudley could have got it out for her long enough to have it copied, except he was in New York and couldn't get away for another week, but he assured her over the phone all the staff was away and told her how to get in.

She went on. "So I came to London with a painter friend of mine named Roberto who's pretty good at that sort of thing——"

Colby interrupted. "Roberto Giannini?"

"That's right. Do you know him?"

"Sure. He was the one who painted it in the first place."

She smiled. "That would have appealed to Roberto, being commissioned to forge his own forgery."

They rented a car and parked near the house a little after midnight. Around in back was a window that could be reached by climbing a drainpipe. She helped boost Roberto up. He opened the window and went in. He had a piece of cord to lower the painting with, and then they'd take it to the hotel where he could work. She waited in the car.

Twenty minutes went by, and he didn't come out. Then an hour. The painting was in the library, on another floor and in a different wing of the house, but he had a flashlight and a sketch, so she didn't see how he could get lost. She began to worry. Calling the police seemed to have little to recommend it under the circumstances, so all she could do was chew her nails and go on waiting. When it began to grow light, she had to leave.

She reached for another herring. Colby waited.

"It was four days before I saw him again," she went on. "He came to the hotel early one morning, and he had the Braque with him. He was pale and jumpy, and kept begging me to put some more clothes on. Roberto's a certified, card-carrying Italian and only twenty-six, so I couldn't figure out what was the matter with him until he told me she'd given him the painting. Also a thirty-acre farm in Tuscany, and a Jaguar."

Miss Manning had come back from Paris, alone, just an hour or so before they'd got there. She caught Roberto taking the Braque down off the wall in the library, and grabbed for the phone to call the police. He didn't want to hurt her, of course, but he didn't want to go to jail, either, so being Italian, he went for the Italian solution.

He wouldn't say much about it, but apparently it was a little hectic in the courtship department, and must have sounded like a remake of *La Ronde* with the Hatfields and McCoys. She began screeching and throwing books at him, and in addition she was wearing a girdle and had one foot caught in a rhinoceros-leg wastebasket. And while it seemed an ambitious undertaking for a man who was scared to death to begin with, to deflower a forty-three-year-old virgin while she was trying to beat his brains out with *The Brothers Karamazov* and Elizabeth Barrett Browning, Roberto was a pretty good boy.

So she didn't call the police. After the third day Roberto began to consider calling them himself, or at least making a run for it during one of the moments she was asleep, but oddly enough he was becoming rather fond of her. She was sweet to him, he told Martine, and so damned grateful. But he did need rest. He was going back, he said, now that he'd delivered the Braque, but first he just wanted to stand around in Dunhill's for a few hours smelling pipe tobacco and men in from the country in damp tweed.

"Anyway, to get to the point," Martine continued, "after making nearly two million dollars writing about sex, she'd finally discovered it. So she quit writing."

"Why?" Colby asked. "Decided it was too much for her?"

"No. She just didn't want to waste the time."

She took off with him. That was seven months ago, and nobody had seen her since. Nor heard from her, except once. From this sole scrap of information, an ecstatic and somewhat incoherent postcard from Samos, she appeared to be cruising the Dodecanese in a chartered yacht, going ashore nights with Roberto to get intoxicated with beauty and laid among the olive groves and ancient marble. And while this sounded like a lot more fun than writing about it, she was going broke, what with income tax and the money she was throwing around. And the trouble was she didn't know it; if she did, she might come back and go to work. Dudley, of course, could probably run her down with private detectives, but he was reluctant to tell her. To a large extent, he was the reason she was broke.

He hadn't actually stolen anything from her, of course. It was just that he had converted four hundred thousand dollars' worth of her bonds to cash and put it into some electronics stock that was going to double overnight.

Colby nodded. He was familiar with the routine, an ancient and deceptively simple one, with a staggering mortality rate. You just put the four hundred thousand back in the bonds, plus normal interest accrual, and pocketed the rest. Only the stock went down instead of up, and the janitor had to clean another mess off the sidewalk in front of the Southbound Fidelity Trust.

"She was lucky to have Dudley taking care of her money, instead of some drunken sailor," he said. "At least she hasn't got a hangover."

"Well, it's not completely lost yet," Martine replied. "The stock may come back eventually, if he could keep stalling an audit."

But in the meantime Miss Manning's checks kept pouring into the bank from Corfu, Athens, Istanbul, Rhodes, and any other place that had night once a day and a double bed. There'd been an eighty-thousand-dollar installment to pay on her income tax in September, and another eighty thousand coming up in January. She didn't have it. So around the fifteenth of January, the balloon was going up for Dudley. But he still had one chance.

"A new book," Colby said.

She nodded. "Shortly after she took off, he found part of a new novel she'd started, and sent it off to her literary agent. It was only about two pages, but they got seven hundred thousand dollars for the reprint rights, and it sold to the movies for half a million. Which wasn't bad, considering. What was it Milton got for *Paradise Lost*?"

"I've forgotten," he said. "Eighteen pounds, wasn't it?"

"Something like that. Anyway, that's the situation. The money's there and waiting, and all he has to do is deliver a novel."

"So he's having one manufactured?"

"Yes. When he'd given up all hope she was ever coming back, he came to me for help. I suggested he farm it out. It's been done before."

"Sure. Dumas *père* used to subcontract plenty of it."

She nodded. "All he had to do was hire a reasonably competent writer, give him copies of her other five books and that two-page outline, and tell him to spread some more flesh on it."

"But what's she going to do when she discovers she's written a new novel?"

"If Roberto can go the distance, she may not find it out for years. And what can she do? Deny she wrote it and give back the money—after Internal Revenue's already got most of it?"

They had a point there, Colby thought. He could see IRS giving it back, whether the book had been written by Petronius Arbiter or G. A. Henty. "How's he making out?"

"Beautifully—until four days ago."

In July, Dudley had gone to New York and located a couple of writers, and brought them back to Paris as a security measure. Naturally, the whole thing had to be kept secret. Miss Manning's literary agent and publisher didn't know she had disappeared, and would go up like Krakatoa if they found out what was going on. Dudley forged her signature on correspondence and contracts. As a team, the two writers clicked from the first minute. Neither could have written it alone—one hadn't written anything in fifteen years and the other had never written fiction at all—but together they rolled it out like toothpaste, and it was pure Manning. In two months they had half of it done. Dudley sent that much of it off to New York, and her agent and publisher raved about it. They said it was the best thing she'd ever done.

"Then what's the problem?" Colby asked. "They must be about finished."

"One of them is, almost. But four days ago the other one just walked out and nobody's seen her since."

"You mean she quit?"

"He doesn't know what happened. They had an argument, and the next morning she wasn't there at breakfast. That wasn't too unusual, she quite often stayed out all night. But she didn't show up at all. Nor the next day."

Dudley couldn't notify the police, because he couldn't very well explain what she was doing there in the house; it might get in the papers. Last night Martine had called Paris and canvassed all the hospitals, since Dudley couldn't speak a word of French, but there was no trace of the girl. Her passport was still there in the house, so she couldn't have left the country, but she might have gone off to the Riviera with some boyfriend.

"Did she take any clothes?"

"He doesn't know. She still has things there, but she could have taken something."

"Sure," he agreed, but still not completely satisfied. Then he shrugged. "But couldn't the other one finish it alone?"

"Only his part of it. I'll have to explain how they worked. Their names are Casey Sanborn and Kendall Flanagan. You've probably never heard of them. I hadn't."

"No," he said. "I don't think so."

Sanborn was an old pulp writer back in the 1930's and '40's who used to turn out three to four million words a year under contract to several strings of magazines and under half a dozen names—sea stories, mysteries, adventure stories, but mostly westerns. He'd hardly written anything since the pulp magazines folded, but when he sat down at a typewriter it sounded like a machine-gunner repelling an attack. He erupted characters and plots like a broken fire main, and of course he had the five Manning novels for a style book, but still it wasn't quite Manning. It

29

wasn't lack of talent, but simply a matter of early conditioning and the fact he was a little too old to adapt.

In the pulps, skin had to be leathery, and nobody ever stroked it—they just shot at it. So Sanborn was never entirely convincing at the silken, magenta-nippled breast; when Derek pressed his face into Gloria's cleavage there was always an impression this didn't quite ring true from a motivational standpoint and he should have been off doing a man's work, shooting Comanches, or helping the boys get the herd to Abilene. And that was where Kendall Flanagan came in.

"She's from Madison Avenue," Martine went on, "and writes toilet soap and skin lotion commercials for TV, all dewy and tremulous and full of ankle-deep adjectives——"

Colby gestured approvingly. "Hey, he's got it."

"Sure. I don't know whether it was accidental or not, but it's the perfect synthesis. They didn't write it *ensemble*. Sanborn'd write it—the whole thing, plot, characters, dialogue, and all—and then turn it over to her and she'd spray on the flesh tones. That is, she'd simply rewrite the same story, but in ad-agency marshmallow, and when it came out of her typewriter you were smothered in skin and Nuit d'Amour and you could hear the nylon slithering to the floor. As her publishers said, it's absolutely topdrawer Manning with the drawer pulled out. But now Flanagan's disappeared, and she had nearly fifty pages to go.

"Merriman can't turn it in like that. So there he sits, with the million dollars practically in the bank, and he can't touch it."

"It could drive him crazy," Colby said.

"It's about to. I went to Lausanne to talk to a writer I know there, but he was busy. There was another here in London, but he'd just gone to work for MGM. So I thought of you. Could you do it?"

Colby thought about it. Vicarious sex bored him to death and he wasn't sure he could write it, but now he'd found her again he couldn't let her get away. "Sure. I mean, if he'll hire both of us."

"Why both of us?"

"I can't spell worth a damn," he explained hastily. "And there's

30

the feminine expertise, like whether you can put a girdle back on in a Volkswagen——"

The telephone rang.

She answered. She listened for a moment, winked at Colby, and said soothingly, "All right, Merriman, just calm down. . . . Oh-oh! . . . Oh, murder! . . . But he's still there? . . . Just a minute. . . ."

She turned to Colby. "Everything's down the drain now. There's a reporter in the house, and he's got the whole story."

I should have asked about the pension plan, he thought. "Let me talk to him."

She handed him the phone. "What paper's this guy with?" he asked.

"Who's this?" Dudley demanded.

"Lawrence Colby. The writer Martine was talking to——"

"*Writer?* What the hell do I want with a writer now? All I need's a good lawyer and a hungry judge——"

"Calm down," Colby said. "What about this reporter?"

"The whole thing's shot to hell!" Dudley was beginning to shout. "Work your fingers to the bone trying to keep her solvent while she chases around the Mediterranean getting banged from Gibraltar to the Nile Hilton!"

"Relax, will you? Where is he now?"

"Locked in the back room of the office. When I found out who he was I got him in there and slammed the door. I thought maybe Martine could think of something."

"Maybe we can. Is there a phone in the room?"

"An extension."

"Has he used it yet?"

"I don't think so. He's just pounding on the door and yelling. Listen."

In the background Colby could hear thuds and muffled protest. The reporter was undoubtedly American; mother-grabber had a nostalgic ring to it. "Can you cut the line?"

"Sure," Dudley said. "I already have. But look—Chrissakes, what can we do now?"

"He can't get out the window?"

"It's on the second floor." There was a wistful flowering of hope in Dudley's voice. "Maybe he'll try it and kill himself."

"Do you know where he's from?"

"Los Angeles. The *Chronicle.*"

"Are you sure he's got the whole story?"

"*The whole story?* The bastard could hang me! Look. . . . He called here yesterday, wanted to arrange an interview. He was on his way home from Berlin or somewhere and stopped off in Paris. He wanted to do a feature article on Sabine Manning, under a by-line, good publicity for her, that pitch. I told him nothing doing, of course, Miss Manning was too busy on her new book. That gets rid of most of 'em, but this bird was a little tougher. He sneaked in through the kitchen this morning, and walked right into the room where Sanborn was working. Oh, sweet Jesus——!"

Colby whistled softly.

"Sanborn just thought he was the new writer I'd been trying to get, so he showed him the manuscript and started to fill him in. By the time I walked in from the airport he had it all, and he started to laugh and said wait'll *this* hits the front page. I tried to buy him off—that's how I got him into the office."

"All right," Colby said. "Keep him locked in there till we can get to Paris. We'll call you from Orly."

"You mean, you think there's something we can do?"

"I don't know yet. But I used to be a——" He turned, intending to motion for Martine to start getting dressed. She already had. "——news——"

She had the garter belt girded around her under the loosened peignoir, and was sitting on the edge of the bed pulling on her nylons. A slender, tapering leg was thrust up and outward, rotating at the ankle as she slid the stocking-top up a satiny expanse of thigh and clipped it to the tab.

"What's the matter?" Dudley demanded. "Have you got asthma?"

"Asthma? No. I'm twenty-twenty in both eyes."

"Oh . . . Martine. I think she grew up on a destroyer. But you used to be a what?"

"A newspaperman," Colby said. An idea was beginning to take form in his mind. "It's just possible we may be able to get that guy out of your hair, but there'll be a slight fee."

"How much?"

"A thousand dollars."

33

"A *thousand!*" Dudley seemed to choke, and began making sputtering noises.

"Plus expenses," Colby went on.

"Five hundred——"

"If he files that story, you know what your manuscript'll be worth?"

"So I know, I know! Okay, a thousand. But no-cure-no-pay."

"Right," Colby agreed. "We'll be in Paris as fast as we can get there. Find out his name and where he's staying. And feed him a sob story. Sabine Manning died of cholera out in some back island of the Cyclades and you were trying to finish the novel she was working on so you can give the money to some charity she was interested in——"

"You want me to tell that to a *reporter?*"

"So let him laugh. When we call you from Orly, answer from some other extension so he can't hear you. . . . Oh, one more thing—that Flanagan girl still hasn't shown up?"

"No. And if I ever get my hands on her——"

"You haven't checked with the police?"

"No."

"She hasn't got her passport with her," Colby pointed out. "If they'd picked her up for anything, they'd hold her till she produced one. Are you sure they haven't tried to call you?"

"Sure I'm sure. They'd speak English, wouldn't they?"

"Not necessarily. They would if they saw they had to."

"That's what I thought. This jerk that keeps bugging me——"

"What?" Colby asked.

"Nothing. Just some flip-lid that keeps calling up here three or four times a day trying to sell me something. In French, for Christ's sake! But never mind him——"

"Wait a minute," Colby broke in. "Tell me about this guy."

"Hell, I don't know anything about him. I got troubles of my own without listening to his, even if I could understand 'em. When I hang up on him, he calls right back and starts blowing his stack all over the place. You know how excitable they are."

"How long has this been going on?"

"Three or four days."

Colby frowned and glanced at Martine. She had her slip on and was pulling her dress over her head. Her face emerged, the eyes questioning. In the receiver he could hear the reporter banging and cursing again.

"Listen," he said to Dudley. "Have you received any mail the past few days?"

"Sure. Piles of it, same as always. Fanmail, begging letters, she gets 'em all the time."

"No, I mean local. In French."

"I might have. Seems to me there was something this morning."

"Have you got it there?"

"No, I probably threw it out. I couldn't read it."

"Will you look in the wastebasket and see if it's still there?"

"What the hell—? Oh, all right. . . ." There was a scrambling sound and a rustling of paper. "Yeah, here it is."

"Can you read it to me?"

"Seems to be addressed to me. *Cher monsewer*, it says——"

"Go on."

"The first two words are *Madame Manning*. I can make that out. Then it says, *ay eat enlevvy*——"

"Hold it, hold it!" Colby interrupted. "Just spell the words."

"Okay. . . . *Madame Manning—a*—that's one word—*e-t-e*—the e's have got accent marks——"

"Right. Go on."

". . . *e-n-l-e-v-é-e*. . . ."

"Okay. That's enough." Colby put his hand over the mouthpiece, and turned to Martine. "They've been trying to tell him for four days they've kidnaped Kendall Flanagan."

"Oh, no!"

"They think she's Miss Manning."

She shook her head and sat down. "You don't suppose President Johnson would declare him a disaster area?"

Colby spoke into the phone again. "The reason your friend's so excitable is frustration. He kidnaped Kendall Flanagan four days ago and can't get anybody to notice it. Is she a heavy eater?"

"*What?*"

"That's right."

"If they're going to kidnap Americans, why the hell don't they learn English?"

"Look at the rest of it. Are there any figures?"

"Yeah. Here's something that looks like one hundred thousand. I guess that's a one in front."

"The European one. Dollars or francs?"

"Dollars—" Dudley did a double take, and gasped. "A hundred thousand dollars? Are they nuts?"

"They think they've got Miss Manning."

"I don't care if they've got the Lido floor show. I haven't got a hundred thousand dollars."

"Okay," Colby said crisply. "You need help, and you need it bad. But one thing at a time. We've got to get to Paris." He glanced at his watch. "We'll see what we can do about that reporter, and then try to be at the house when your friend calls again. We should be able to make it before five p.m. If he calls before we get there, keep saying *rappelez à cinq heures—rappelez à cinq heures*. Can you do that?"

"*Rappley a sank ur.* I can remember it."

"Good. If he knows he's finally going to get through to somebody, he won't kill her before five o'clock anyway."

"You think they might do that?"

"They will if they don't get some action. They didn't plan on seeing her through to Medicare. We'll call you from Orly."

He hung up and turned to Martine. Her eyes were blazing with excitement and curiosity. "Zip me up and brief me," she said.

"They want a hundred thousand——" he said, yanking up the zipper.

"*Ouch!* No wonder you're divorced."

"I'm sorry." He worked the zipper back and freed the strand of dark hair caught in the top of it. "Both my wives were bald."

"They were if they were married to you very long. But about the reporter, and the kidnapers——"

As briefly as he could, he told her the essentials, and headed for the door. "Ask your concierge to reserve us space on the next flight to Paris. Grab a taxi, and pick me up at the Green Park."

"Right. Have you got any ideas?"

"I'm working on one." He waved and went out.

He was pacing the sidewalk in front of his hotel twenty minutes later when she drew up in a taxi. He threw his bag in front beside the driver and jumped in. They shot ahead.

"There's a flight at eleven-ten," she said, glancing at her watch. "The driver thinks we can just about make it." They circled the block and slid back into the traffic of Piccadilly. She brought out cigarettes. Colby lighted hers and one for himself. "All right," she urged. "What are we going to do?"

"The newspaperman's the first thing," he replied. "We've got to keep him from filing that story."

"How? She's a big name, remember."

"First I need a little rundown on the house, layout, who's in it, and so on."

Martine had been in it a number of times. It was a big three-story place in the sixteenth *arrondissement* near the Avenue Victor Hugo. Sabine Manning's study, bedroom, and bath were on the ground floor, in addition to the salon, dining room, and kitchen. Sanborn's and Kendall Flanagan's rooms were on the second floor, as well as Dudley's office and the room behind it in which the reporter was locked. The window of this room was at the back of the house. He wouldn't be able to see the street.

The only other people were a housekeeper and a cook, both hired by Dudley. Miss Manning's secretary had quit about the time she took off, and he'd never replaced her. The cook was a Gascon, and the housekeeper a Parisienne named Madame Buffet. The cook could speak no English at all, but Madame Buffet knew a few words.

Colby nodded, his eyes thoughtful. "Good. We may be able to do it. With luck."

"How does it work?"

"If it does." He explained the idea.

She listened with increasing, and unholy, glee. "This is going to be fun." Then her face sobered. "But what about the other thing?"

"Considerably less fun, and somebody may get hurt," he said.

37

"A lot depends on what they do when they find out they've got the wrong woman."

Their flight was already being announced when he paid off the taxi and they ran into the terminal, but they were able to pick up their tickets, check in, and clear passport control in time to get aboard. When they were airborne, Colby lighted a cigarette and turned to Martine.

"Do you live in Geneva?"

"No, Paris. An apartment near the Étoile."

"We're neighbors, then. I live on the Avenue Kléber. How long have you been in Paris?"

"I was born there," she said. "But the question isn't how long, but how often."

"How's that?"

"My father was American, and my mother French. I grew up like a migratory waterfowl—a victim of a sort of bilaterally expatriated chauvinism."

"Maybe you'd better throw in a glossary with that," he said.

She explained. Her father, the son of a midwestern businessman, had come to Paris just out of college in 1934 to study painting for a year. He'd never amounted to much as a painter, but he had become enamored of Paris and refused to go home. Fortunately, he inherited some money from his maternal grandfather, and didn't have to. He married a minor French actress originally from Bordeaux, and Martine was born in 1936. When the Germans came, he sent his wife and daughter off to the United States and joined the Resistance, and then later the OSS, still working with the French underground. When it was over they were reunited in Paris. Only now the American was more French than the French themselves, and the Frenchwoman had eaten Mom's apple pie. Live in this place? Dear, you need help.

They were both people of volcanic temperament, given to violent separations and unpredictable reconciliations that never lasted long because she refused to give up the fat-cat life of plush suburbia and he was too furiously intent on dragging France back into *la belle époque* even to consider going home and abandoning it to its fate. He'd saved it from the Germans, and now if necessary he'd save it from the French.

Martine shuttled back and forth on the shockwaves of these domestic upheavals, attending school in Paris and St. Louis, and Paris and Phoenix, and Paris and Palm Beach, and later, when she was older and they had split up permanently, boarding school in Switzerland and England. She developed the DP's honed and polished instinct for survival, finding that she could assimilate a language and a culture apparently through her pores and fit into an alien environment with the ease of a Greek or a Polish Jew, so she was never the "new kid" anywhere more than a few weeks.

"If they'd sent me off to school with a bunch of Kurdish tribesmen," she said, "I'd have been cooking over a camel-dung fire on the second day, speaking the local dialects in a month, and had solid connections in the dung black-market at the end of two." She discovered she was a born operator.

"My father's dead now," she went on, "and my mother's married to a real-estate developer in the San Fernando Valley. She drives a Cadillac about a foot longer than a *bateau-mouche*, saves fourteen different kinds of trading stamps, belongs to the John Birch Society, and would have to be in surgery to miss *The Beverly Hillbillies*. And if my father were still alive—what with a drugstore on the Champs Élysées, the language filling up with *franglais*, and people drinking *weesky*—he'd probably be living somewhere in the provinces in an abandoned mill like Daudet, and doing translations of Rimbaud. So with a French mother who was American and an American father who was French, I was never sure who I was." She smiled, and gestured humorously. "Except maybe a refugee."

"What do you do now?" Colby asked.

"I play a small part in a film now and then, and do an odd job occasionally for a friend of mine who runs a detective agency."

They were down at Orly and cleared through Customs at twelve-thirty P.M. They located an unoccupied telephone *cabine*. While Colby searched for a *jeton* among the Swiss, French, and English coins in his pockets, she dug a small address book from her purse. He dialed.

"Hello, hello!" Dudley barked.

"This is Colby. Has he called again?"

"Yeah. About twenty minutes ago. I gave him the *rappley a sank ur* business, and I think he understood. But why in hell didn't they get her to call, if they couldn't speak English?"

"They're calling from a public phone. But let's get to the first job. You've still got him?"

"Yeah. He's quiet now; he's broken all the chairs on the door and given up. His name's Moffatt, and he's staying at the George V."

"The George V? He's not a newspaperman, he's a journalist."

"He's a no-good bastard. Okay, what else?"

"Go up to the office where he can hear you," Colby said. "Pretend to call Air France, and make a reservation on the next flight to Brazil or Outer Mongolia or anywhere there's no extradition for fraud. Make it good, you're taking it on the lam——"

"What's all this for?"

Colby cut him off. "Don't argue, and don't ask questions. We haven't got time for explanations. We'll take a cab from here. Watch for us. When we go past the house we'll wave. Then I want you to let him escape."

"*Escape?* Are you nuts? He'll——"

"Stop interrupting. And when I say escape, I mean escape. He'll bribe his way out. Tell the housekeeper to go up there and stooge around the outer office with a carpet sweeper or something so he'll know it's not you."

"I'm not sure I can explain all that to her."

"Then just tell her to come to the door when we get there."

"Okay. What else?"

"As soon as he's out of the house, start calling the George V at about five-minute intervals with messages for a Miss Nadja Loring. She's due there for lunch. Have her paged."

"What kind of messages, and who from?"

"From anybody. The Coast is trying to get her, London's been on the horn all morning, don't forget the appointment at Balmain, call Liz and Dick—you know the drill, break out the rubber boots and shovels."

40

"Anything else?"

"Just a description."

"His mother's probably cut her throat because they didn't get the pills on the market in time——"

"No, I mean, what does he look like?"

"Big beefy bastard about fifty or fifty-five, lot of grayish-red hair, and a nose like a neon pineapple."

"Right. Watch for us."

He hung up and turned to Martine. "Have you got any sunglasses?"

"For a trip to London? I'll pick up a pair at one of the shops while you're calling the dog man. Here's some more *jetons*."

She left. Colby looked up the number in his address book. André Michod, who ran a small bookshop in the Boulevard Raspail, owned a pair of borzois he rented to studios. Madame answered. Yes, Sacha and Dmitri were at liberty and could be engaged for the afternoon. She would have them brushed and ready. In about twenty minutes, Colby said. He hung up and dialed Bill Elkins.

Bill was an old friend, an ex-newspaper photographer turned free lance. There was no answer at his apartment. Colby tried his alternate business address, the café across the street. Monsieur Elkins? *Mais oui. Ne quittez pas.* . . . Bill came on. He sounded sober, and wasn't doing anything at the moment.

"I've got a job for you," Colby said. "A hundred francs, and it'll take about an hour."

"What's the average prison term if I get caught?"

"It's perfectly legal."

"I suppose it could happen. Okay, what do I photograph?"

"Nothing. I just want somebody who looks like a photographer."

"Oh, I do, I do."

"Show up in front of the George V in about thirty minutes loaded down with gear—couple of cameras, lens cases, tripod, flash-holders, the works. Just wait there. Pretty soon you'll see me go in the entrance, and right behind me a very pretty girl will get out of a taxi. You come in with her——"

"Then the lights go out, and when they come back on, I'm

41

dancing with Fidel Castro and you've got the babe. I've been through this before."

"No. You make the entrance with her, and stay with her. You've been with her all morning. Catch?"

"Okay. How do I recognize her?"

"Watch carefully for a tall, beautiful brunette wearing dark glasses and a natural mink coat and leading a pair of Russian wolfhounds."

"What color wolfhounds?"

"Shut up and listen, I haven't got much time. You'll join me inside—in the bar, I hope. Take your cues from us, and play it off the board. You won't have to say much."

"Who's all this for?"

"A newspaperman named Moffatt, a big guy with a red nose. You don't know him."

"No. But I probably will. I hope he dances a slow foxtrot."

"See you in forty minutes to an hour." Colby hung up. Martine was hurrying toward him. They ran for the exits.

It was one of those afternoons Colby loved best in Paris, that rare October day when it wasn't raining and the Automobile Show had already closed. In autumn's golden haze there was an Impressionist softening of form and line, and the chestnut trees were beginning to turn.

Number 7 Rue des Feuilles Mortes was a block and a half from the Avenue Victor Hugo, just beyond the Rue Ciel Bleu, a massive gray stone house with a slate roof. The taxi, with Colby alone in the back seat, slid to the curb and stopped. Colby looked back. The other taxi, which they'd picked up in the Boulevard Raspail, was just turning into the street. It came on past with Martine sharing the rear seat with Sacha and Dmitri, who looked out at the sixteenth *arrondissement* with patrician calm, appreciative but not overawed. It turned right at the next corner and disappeared.

Colby took the two bags, told the driver to wait, and went up the steps. He rang the bell. Almost immediately, the heavy carved door jerked open, and he was face to face with a woman who seemed to be violently in motion while standing still, like a hummingbird. She would have been hard pushed to weigh eighty pounds, even with the Disque Bleu dangling from the corner of her mouth, and might have been anywhere between thirty and fifty years of age. Brown eyes regarded him with the Parisienne's compound of warmth and humor and total lack of illusion about anything whatever.

But of course, she said in a husky voice, Monsieur Colby's arrival had been awaited. She was Madame Buffet. Colby smiled and said he was enchanted. She threw the bags behind her into the doorway, and he touched on the affair of the prisoner.

Oh, yes, one hears the outcries, and one senses he is a prisoner strongly discontented with all aspects of the situation, but. . . .

She shrugged. Happy prisoners were probably rare anywhere. Colby gathered she had work of her own to do without getting involved in American activities like trapping each other, and in any event nothing that happened in this household would ever surprise her in the slightest. When, however, he outlined just how the prisoner was to be allowed to escape, her interest quickened. Yes, of course she could understand one hundred francs spoken in English. Also two hundred. Who knows, maybe he would bring five hundred, if allowed to age a little more.

No, Colby said, the essential was to harvest him as quickly as possible; price was secondary. While he wouldn't dream of subjecting her to the humiliation of taking the first offer, she must limit the negotiations to a maximum of three minutes. She agreed, though somewhat reluctantly. And now—about splitting the take? It was all hers, Colby said, and realized at once this was probably a tactical error.

Her eyes narrowed and she was instantly on guard. Why would the Americans go to all the trouble to trap the pigeon and then toss the profits away? Colby hastened to explain. This was merely the opening move in a more complicated affair; the pigeon had to be allowed to escape in order that the further developments could unroll themselves. Aaaah! One comprehends. Then the thing to do was get him out forthwith, and perhaps they would set the trap again. Exactly, Colby said.

Writing books seemed to be an interesting field in America, she observed; one had a little difficulty at times in following the process, but it was lively. It was no wonder the *Série Noire* published so many of them. Well, if Monsieur Colby was ready, she would throw out the first pigeon.

Colby thanked her and went back to the taxi. He directed the chauffeur to go on to the next corner and turn right. Here, in the Rue Mon Coeur, Martine's taxi was parked at the opposite curb, just back from the corner so as to be out of sight of anyone emerging from the house. They made a U-turn and parked behind it. He got out and walked forward.

"From Dudley's description," he said, "the chances are he'll

44

head for the bar to write it. A nose like that takes a lot of maintenance."

She winked and nodded. He walked up to the corner and looked down along the Rue des Feuilles Mortes toward the taxi stand on the opposite side of the Avenue Victor Hugo. There were two taxis in it at the moment. Nothing stirred along the street. He lighted a cigarette and waited several minutes.

Then suddenly the door of Number 7 burst open, and a big, rumpled-looking man lunged down the steps and turned toward the avenue with the shambling run of a bear. He looked around once, but Colby ducked back out of sight. Colby held up circled thumb and forefinger to Martine behind him, and looked again. Moffatt was crossing the avenue. He got into the Citroën at the head of the taxi station. Colby was already gesturing for his. It came up abreast of him, and he got in just as the Citroën disappeared from view.

When they emerged on the avenue, the Citroën was a couple of blocks ahead. Colby leaned forward and pointed it out to the driver. They settled in behind it, not getting too close, and Colby turned to look back. Martine's taxi was turning in behind them.

They closed up a little as they entered the great interweaving whirlpool of traffic in the Étoile. There were a half-dozen Citroën taxis in sight now, but Colby kept his eyes riveted on the one Moffatt was in. It turned down the Champs Élysées, taking the extreme right lane. There was no doubt now Moffatt was headed for the hotel, just as he had gambled. When they turned into the Avenue George V, Martine's taxi was the second car behind them.

Moffatt's taxi pulled up before the hotel entrance and he leaped out before the doorman could even reach it. Colby leaned forward and paid the driver as his taxi came to a stop, and was out and crossing the sidewalk by the time Moffatt had disappeared inside. Bill Elkins, draped with photographic equipment, was off to his right, boredly watching traffic. He glanced at Colby with no sign of recognition, a large young man with a broken nose and an air of ageless disillusion.

Colby hurried in the entrance. Moffatt was at the concierge's desk, picking up telegraph blanks. Which way would he go, toward the elevators or the bar? Colby glanced behind him. Martine and the wolfhounds were being assisted from the taxi by the doorman and a chasseur, and Bill had already converged on her. They were right on cue. Moffatt turned away from the concierge's desk, toward the bar. Somewhere toward the dining room a chasseur was paging Mademoiselle Loring.

The bar was about half full. Moffatt had taken a table near the far corner and was in conversation with a waiter. The waiter departed. He unclipped a pen, bent over the telegraph blanks, and began furiously writing. Colby sat down two tables away, facing the entrance with his back to the reporter. Moffatt paid no attention.

Martine slipped in with the quiet unobtrusiveness of an ice-show finale, preceded by the wolfhounds and followed by the camera-laden Elkins, turning to call "Here, *garsong*" to the chasseur paging Mademoiselle Loring, and then back to wave and shriek a greeting to Colby. "There's Lawrence now. Are we late, darling?"

Colby stood up, leaned in over the wolfhounds to kiss her, and asked, "Nadja, honey. How'd it go this morning?" By now a waiter was hovering on the perimeter of all this confusion, and the chasseur was holding out the telephone slip. Colby took it, tossed him a franc, glanced at it, and went on without even a pause: "It's Stillman, in London. I'll call him myself, after lunch. It's about the Manning tie-in. What'll you have? And how about you, Bill baby?"

They sat down, Martine opposite him, facing Moffatt's table, and ordered Scotch. Martine took out a cigarette. Colby lighted it for her. "Paris is a doll," she said. "I've looked at so many statues I feel like a caretaker at Forest Lawn."

"You get some pretty good stuff?" Colby asked Elkins.

The latter shrugged. "The usual—the eternal wonder of Paris, youth, innocence, dewy-eyed enchantment——"

"You'd have died!" Martine laughed and tugged the ears of one of the wolfhounds. "I was posing in front of this kooky statue, and Dmitri wanted to lay a dachshund. Talk about on water skis!"

"Now, this afternoon——" Colby began.

Martine interrupted. "I'm dying to hear about the Manning thing."

Colby shot a quick glance around the bar and spoke in a lower tone, but one that could still be overheard from Moffatt's table. "We're in, baby. It's so perfect I get gooseflesh."

The tip of her shoe found his and pressed. They had the Moffatt ear. She had removed her glasses, and now she gazed at him wide-eyed. "She really fell for it?"

"She? Oh, that bubble-headed girl from the Tulsa paper." Colby dismissed her with a wave of the hand. "Honey, you've been out of touch all morning, you haven't heard the word. We did even better. Before she could show up, we hooked a real man-sized chump with circulation."

"Who?"

"Some joker named Muffett or Moffatt, from the *Los Angeles Chronicle*. He just walked in on the setup, cold, and went for it like some kid from the *Pleasanton Weekly Argus*."

"Oooooh, wonderful! And he's already sent in the story?"

"No, no, of course not. Dudley's got him locked in the house——"

"But why?" She shook her head in baffled wonder. "Lawrence, it's *so* complicated."

He sighed. "Look, baby, honey, Nadja darling—the *Chronicle's* an afternoon paper, and there's the difference in time——"

"Doll," Elkins said. "See? You've got this orange here, and over here's a candle, and the orange is turning——"

"Oh, I know about that," she said. "It gets late earlier in Los Angeles than it does here. Or is it early later?"

"That's it! You've got it," Elkins approved. "Astronomers call it the Yogi Berra Effect."

"Dudley's selling him the clincher," Colby explained. "He's pretending to hold him there so he can make it onto a plane for Brazil before the story breaks. Actually, of course, the idea is to keep him from filing the story until just before deadline of today's final, so they won't have time to check with the embassy in Athens to see if some American named Manning did die in the Cyclades. So they'll run the story without the check, because if Dudley's taking it on the lam it's bound to be true.

47

"The wire services will pick it up, and the morning papers can't check with the embassy either, because it'll be closed. So the wire services and all the papers that have Paris bureaus will be calling the house here and sending men around. No answer. Nothing. So it's true, and Dudley's flown the coop. So the morning papers will run it. Boy, the headlines! *Best-selling Author Dead. Fraud Suspected.*

"Then about this time tomorrow, when somebody finally does get in the house, here's Manning typing away to beat hell on another door-stopper, laying 'em three to a page. What's all the uproar? Of course she didn't answer the phone, she never does when she's working. And her secretary was off last night.

"Other writers? Here? Dudley? What drunk poured that one out of a bottle? Dudley's not even in Paris; he's in New York.

"So all the papers that ran the original story will run a re-traction, and there'll be fifty to a hundred that didn't run it the first time that will now because they can't resist the temptation to quote Mark Twain——"

"Isn't that the living *end*?" Martine caught Elkins' arm and cooed with admiration. "Who's Mark Twain?"

"The book goes on sale day after tomorrow," Colby went on, "right in the middle of it, with a big ad campaign. And in our shy little way we break down and admit that Rumford Produc-tions has bought the motion-picture rights and that it's going to be your first starring vehicle, and it just happens we have all those stills of you and Manning discussing the role in the old book-lined study around the famous typewriter—" He paused, shaking his head with wonder. "Brother. It gets you, right in here."

Martine's eyes were suddenly filled with bathos. "But, Law-rence, what about this poor Mr. Muffett? He might have kiddies. Won't he lose his job?"

"So we'll send him a Christmas basket," Colby said. "Look, he'll get another job. . . ."

A chair scraped behind him, and then a shoe. I hope the waiter didn't leave a bottle on his table, he thought. Then he was looking up into a beefy face dominated by its landmark of a nose and a very nasty expression. Moffatt was standing at his left, leaning over the table with the telegraph forms in his hand.

"I was just wondering if I couldn't buy you charming people a drink," he said. "I'm Moffatt of the *Pleasanton Weekly Argus*."

Colby stared in confusion. "What? Moffatt? Now wait a minute, let's don't get excited——"

Moffatt grinned evilly. "Aw, come on, let me sweeten your drink for you, Lawrence baby."

He ripped the telegraph forms to shreds, wadded them, and shoved them into Colby's glass. One strip still dangled over the side. He lifted it between thumb and forefinger, dropped it in, and poked it down carefully into the whiskey and ice.

"Now, look——!" Colby protested.

"And I'll tell you about the *Chronicle*," Moffatt rasped. "Sabine Manning and your friend Dewy-Eyes wouldn't get two lines back in the truss ads if they jumped off the Eiffel Tower with Mao Tse-tung. See you around, Lawrence baby."

He went out. Martine and Colby looked at each other, and she closed one eye in a solemn wink.

"I knew I should have had my silicone injection," Elkins said. "He didn't ask me to dance."

They paid off Elkins and returned the wolfhounds to the Boulevard Raspail. It was three-ten P.M. when they entered the office on the second floor of the house at 7 Rue des Feuilles Mortes. Dudley was on the phone, talking to his stockbroker in New York. He covered the mouthpiece and looked up with the expression of a prisoner watching the jury file in. Martine held up circled thumb and forefinger. He closed his eyes for a second, sighed, and spoke into the telephone again, a man running eternally across a river in desperate leaps from one sinking ice-floe to the next.

". . . all right, sell that fifty shares of DuPont and one hundred of Eastern Airlines, and deposit the proceeds to her account at Chase Manhattan. She seems to like the color of their checks this week, or she's used up the Irving Trust checkbook——"

He sat at a big desk with his back to the nylon-curtained window, a man around fifty with a bony, almost cadaverous face and small glinting eyes the color of topaz. The corner of his mouth twitched as he talked, and he had a nervous habit of running a forefinger inside the collar of his shirt while he thrust out his jaw and craned his neck as though he were choking. He abandoned this long enough to wave for them to sit down, and then grabbed up a cigar from the ashtray in front of him. He puffed furiously three or four times, throwing up a screen of smoke like a beleaguered cuttlefish fleeing its enemies.

Colby looked curiously around the room. Besides the desk it contained several steel filing cabinets, an armchair, and a long deal table piled with unopened mail. On the floor in a corner at the back of the room there were two large cardboard boxes also filled with letters. There was another doorway opposite the one at which they had come in, and through it he could see another, smaller desk and the shattered remains of two chairs lying on the rug.

Martine sat down in the armchair, draping the mink across the back. Colby shoved some of the mail aside and perched on the corner of the table. Dudley was still barking into the telephone. On the desk in front of him were several cablegrams, some opened letters, a bundle of canceled checks three or four inches thick held together by rubber bands, an open ledger, and two stacks of what looked like typing paper held down by onyx paperweights. One was quite small, but the other appeared to be several hundred sheets. Colby looked at it with interest, turned, and met Martine's eyes. She nodded. This was the famous manuscript.

". . . all right, cable me the exact amount of the deposit. G'bye." Dudley hung up. He ground a palm across his face, picked up one of the cablegrams in a hand that trembled slightly, and muttered, ". . . three thousand . . . one thousand eight hundred . . . seven hundred . . . Mother of God. . . ."

Then in a continuation of the same gesture, he threw down the cablegram and stood up. "You really got rid of him? How did you do it? And you're Crosby?"

"Mr. Colby," Martine corrected. "Mr. Dudley."

"Yeah, yeah, sure, I mean Colby." He held out his hand. "But how'd you do it?" he repeated.

"Shall I?" Martine asked.

"Sure," Colby said. He perched on the corner of the table again, lighted a cigarette, and found an ashtray among the mass of letters. Martine told the story, and went on, "——at the moment, the only way Sabine Manning could get her name in the *Los Angeles Chronicle* would be to buy it. So now if you'll write out a check for one thousand thirty-six dollars and fifty cents, we'll get on to your real trouble."

"For a job that took a little over an hour," Dudley said bitterly. "I'm in the wrong line of work."

"We're all in the wrong line of work," she replied, "except Sabine Manning. Shell out, Merriman."

Colby had been staring at the two piles of manuscript on the desk. He could resist it no longer. He stepped over, and asked Dudley, "Do you mind if I look at it?"

"No, go ahead. The thick one. The other's Sanborn's draft."

"He's already finished?" Martine asked.

"About an hour ago. He just left for Orly."

Colby picked up the big stack of sheets, hefted it, and turned it wonderingly in his hands. "I always wanted to feel a million dollars."

Martine smiled and gestured with the cigarette. "A million dollars less fifty pages. At the moment it's not worth ten."

The sheets were blank side up. Colby turned over the top one and looked at the number in the upper right corner. Three hundred and forty-seven.

"Call it four hundred when it's finished," he said, and did a rapid calculation, "Twenty-five hundred dollars a page." Glancing down, he read the last two or three lines.

> She gave a little moan of ecstasy under the pressure of his lips and the age-old feel of the weight, the sweet, smooth, hard, nipple-pressing, thigh-clasped, thrusting male weight of him that. . . .

He balanced the page in his fingers and then put it carefully down on top of the pile. "Two thousand five hundred dollars," he said reverently. And tonight he might get himself killed for two pages of it.

Dudley located the letter among the papers on his desk. It was written in longhand on cheap stationery, and contained little they didn't already know. Madame Manning had been kidnaped, they wanted one hundred thousand dollars, and she would be killed if the police were called in. They would telephone again, and there had better be someone who spoke French.

"Not much to go on, is there?" Martine said.

"No," Colby replied. "Except it's in longhand."

"Plus the fact they got the wrong woman. Probably new at it?"

"Looks that way. Not that that makes 'em any less dangerous." There was more chance his idea would work, but greenhorns were also more likely to panic than professionals. If one of them hit the button, he and Kendall Flanagan would probably be dead.

"What do we do?" Dudley asked.

"The only thing we can do. Negotiate."

"She hasn't got——"

Colby interrupted. "That's what I mean. Neither side has what he's supposed to have. Sabine Manning hasn't got a hundred thousand dollars, and they haven't got Sabine Manning. So it'd be a standoff, except for the fact that the easiest way out for them is to kill her. She might identify them."

"But we're not going to the police," Dudley put in. "We can't."

"They don't know that. I may be able to convince 'em, but don't bet on it. If we get her back, she can finish the novel—in how long?"

"Five days. Maybe less."

"Your manuscript's worth nothing the way it is, and it's also worth nothing if any of this ever gets in the papers. So potentially she's worth a million dollars to you if we can get her back alive and without any publicity. What's Sabine Manning worth at the moment?"

Dudley gave a short, bitter laugh, and dropped into the chair behind the desk. He grabbed up and slammed down the bale of canceled checks, and waved the cablegrams. "If you find out, tell me. It's my job to know what her net worth is from one day to the next, and you know how I do it? I look in tea leaves and chicken entrails——"

"Just calm down, Merriman," Martine soothed.

"Checks!" he groaned. "Have you got any idea how long it takes a check to clear New York from some goat-infested rock in the Aegean that nobody's even heard of since the Trojan War? Or how many of 'em can be in the pipeline at any one time with that woman loose with two checkbooks and a yacht and a coin-operated stallion?"

"Can you make a rough guess?" Colby asked.

"Yeah. There's a Paris *Herald-Tribune* just behind you on that table. Pass me the financial section."

Colby removed the financial page and handed it over. Dudley took from the desk another ledger, a slide rule, and a scratchpad. Muttering to himself, he began making computations, consulting the cablegrams and yesterday's closing Stock Exchange prices. Colby leafed through the rest of the paper, and was folding it to put it aside when his eye was caught by a name on the front page. MYSTERY GIRL SOUGHT IN TORREON SLAYING. It was local. Could they mean Pepe? He quickly read the lead.

> *Police investigating the bizarre slaying five days ago of Jose (Pepe) Torreon, South American millionaire, playboy, and political exile——*

"Hey," he said to Martine, "they got Pepe Torreon."

"Yes, hadn't you heard?" she replied. "He was killed in his apartment with something that looked like a bolt from a crossbow."

> *——are intensifying their search for an unidentified girl described only as being tall, blonde, and apparently Anglo-Saxon——*

54

"Sixty-seven thousand, four hundred eighty-one dollars and fourteen cents," Dudley's voice broke in, "at the close of business in New York yesterday afternoon. But the bank'll be open again in another nineteen minutes." He shuddered.

"How fast can you get hold of ten thousand?" Colby asked.

"There's that much in the Paris account. She hasn't got a checkbook for that one."

"Good. We may be able to swing it for that, or maybe less. However, there's another charge."

"I know," Dudley said wearily. "You and Martine."

"Right. That'll be five thousand."

Dudley groaned, but reached for the checkbook. "Make it payable to Martine. She can give me her check later. The total amount is six thousand thirty-six dollars and fifty cents."

Martine put the check in her purse. Colby looked at his watch. "You and Martine go to the bank. I'll stick by the phone. Get fifty thousand francs, nothing bigger than hundreds and no new bills with consecutive numbers. Then stop at a kiosk or bookstore and get a good map of the city and a Michelin road map of France. Martine can go by her apartment on the way back and pick up her car."

They left. The house was silent except for the humming of Madame Buffet's vacuum cleaner somewhere on the lower floor. He paced the office, trying not to think of how hairy it could get if something went wrong. To take his mind off it, he leafed through a few of the manuscript's sizzling love scenes, and turned up a page of Sanborn's version to see what it was like.

and then with a shy little smile she was fumbling with the straps and buckles. The negligee slipped from her body and she stood before him completely nude, glossy, deep-chested, clean-limbed, her conformation impossible to fault. His heart leaped. . . .

He ought to get a bet down on her before the windows closed, Colby thought. There wasn't much doubt it needed the Flanagan touch to whip it into final shape. After four o'clock he began to check the time every few minutes. It was four-twenty . . . four-thirty-five. . . . At four-forty Dudley came in carrying the two maps and a briefcase bulging with francs. Colby checked the money. It was all right. As he was closing the briefcase they heard the tapping of heels in the hallway. Martine came in. She had changed into a severe dark suit that looked like Balenciaga, and in place of the mink was wearing a cloth coat that was probably easier to drive in. It was obvious from her expression that she had news.

"I just saw Roberto," she said.

Dudley whirled. *"What?"*

"I'm sorry. But it was Roberto. I was going up the Champs Élysées in a taxi, and he was on the curb waiting to cross. He saw me, too, and we waved, but I couldn't stop."

"She wasn't——?" Dudley swallowed and tried again. "You didn't see——?"

"No. There was a woman with him, but it wasn't Miss Manning. Much younger. But if she's not with him, where is she?"

Colby frowned. Maybe she *was* dead. Could somebody be forging the checks? "Are you sure it's her signature?" he asked Dudley, and then realized it was a superfluous question. If Dudley was forging it himself he must know it when he saw it.

"Oh, it's hers. Nobody could fool a bank with that many."

"And they're all cashed in the Aegean area?"

"Aegean and eastern Mediterranean. And always in seaports. That's why we thought she was still on that yacht with Roberto." His eyes had taken on a haunted look. "God, she might walk in here any minute."

"We haven't got time to dream up new disasters," Colby broke in. "We're going to get plenty of argument over the identification, so I'll need Kendall Flanagan's passport and something with Manning's picture on it. How about book jackets?"

"There's a couple that have it."

"And she and Flanagan don't look anything alike?"

"That doesn't scratch the surface," Martine said. "Kendall's fifteen years younger and a blonde."

"Okay. Let's clear this desk."

They cleaned it off and unfolded the maps. Colby set a scratch-pad and pencil within reach, and sat down. "No English," he said to Dudley. "If he hears things going on in a language he doesn't understand, he may spook."

"Is your French as good as Martine's?" Dudley asked. "Maybe she ought to do the talking."

"Hers is too good; she has no accent at all. He'll know I'm an American, which is just what I want. We need leverage."

Dudley looked questioning, but said nothing further. Martine pulled over the armchair and sat down at Colby's right. All three were looking at their watches. It was five to five . . . two minutes to five. . . . Colby could feel the old tightness in his chest the way it was over Korea just before the jump, and didn't like it. Everything depended on his getting the upper hand, and he had to keep any trace of nervousness out of his voice.

The telephone rang. They all started. He took out a cigarette, and let it ring twice more before he picked it up. "Allo."

"Allo! Allo! Do you speak French?" It was a young man's voice, and sounded excited and angry.

"Yes." Colby leaned back casually in the swivel chair. It squeaked. He clicked the cigarette lighter near the mouthpiece and fired up the cigarette. "I speak French."

"Well, at last. Who are you?"

"My name is Colby. I work for a friend of Sabine Manning, in Chicago."

"Aha! But if you're from Cheek-ago, how do you speak French so well?"

"I speak French with an accent. You know that."

"Yes, truly, an accent. But not so bad. Not like Cheek-ago."

"I lived in France for many years," Colby said. "I was the agent for my—ah—company, in Marseille."

"What company?"

"You ask too many questions," he said, suddenly brusque. "We're wasting time, and you've already made enough mistakes." He saw Martine, at the end of the desk, smile and hold up crossed fingers.

57

"What do you mean, mistakes?" This sounded like bluster. Good.

"You snatched an American, and not one of your mob speaks English. You didn't half case the job, so you got the wrong woman——"

"She's not the wrong woman. Don't try——"

"Suppose you let me finish," he broke in curtly. "And then on top of everything else, you sent the note in your own handwriting. You might as well have signed your name. But don't worry about it," he added in the weary tone of one long accustomed to coping with subordinates' blunders. "I'll get it back to you."

"We have Madame Manning——"

"*Mademoiselle* Manning is forty-three years old, a brunette, and is in the Aegean islands. The woman you have is a twenty-eight-year-old blonde named Kendall Flanagan. Surely she's told you this."

"So she says. But everybody knows writers use other names on their books."

"You don't think I'd be stupid enough to tell you this unless I intended to furnish proof, do you? We're wasting time arguing about it. However, I'll explain the whole thing to you, just once, and then I'll tell you what I've been authorized to do.

"This young lady is a friend of Mademoiselle Manning, and also a friend of the man I work for in Chicago. For—uh—health reasons, she had to leave Chicago for awhile, so Mademoiselle Manning, who as I said was away in the Greek islands, offered her the use of her house here in Paris. When she disappeared four days ago, Monsieur Dudley, the man you tried to talk to, was very worried, knowing about her delicate health, so he cabled my boss in Chicago.

"Normally, the man who's in charge of our operation in Marseille would have come up to look into it, but he'd just had an accident in Istanbul, and was in the hospital. So my boss sent for me to come over. I'd have been here yesterday, but I was cooling another beef in Las Vegas. But never mind that. . . . While I was waiting for the plane in New York, I called Monsieur Dudley, who read me your note. So I called my boss. He was

—uh—upset over the news, but I managed to convince him it might be better to let me handle it this way. Alone, you know what I mean?

"The syndi—I mean, company—doesn't want to get mixed up in anything that might cause a lot of stink and start rocking the boat—you know, unfavorable publicity—so seeing it was just a mistake on your part, we'll buy a piece of your action, but not at anything like the price you're talking about. As soon as I'm satisfied Mademoiselle Flanagan hasn't been mistreated in any way, I'll turn over to you thirty thousand francs——"

"Thirty thousand *francs*? You think we are children?"

"My advice, friend, would be to take it."

"This is—how do you call it—chicken food."

"And it will be paid only after I see Mademoiselle Flanagan myself."

"See her? Are you crazy?"

"Wait a minute!" Colby said ominously. "She *is* all right, isn't she? If anything has happened to her——"

"Nothing has happened. She is quite well, and has already cost us a fortune in food and wine. But *see her*? You think you can come out here?"

"What's the problem?" Colby asked. "We just set up a Healy."

"A what?"

"A Healy Pickup. . . . Listen, who's in charge of your operation? Maybe I'd better talk to him."

"I am in charge."

"Oh? And you've never used a Healy? But never mind, I'll explain it to you. You choose the time and place—it'll be night, of course, and the best place is a country road.

"I'll be alone and unarmed, walking along the left side of the road, going in the direction you tell me. When you come up behind me, you already know there are no cars parked back in that direction, so you go on past for another mile or so to be sure there's no muscle or any fuzz staked out ahead. Then you come back. I can't see you, naturally, because your headlights are in my eyes. You stop. I turn around, facing away from the car, with my hands on top of my head. You cover, make the frisk, and put

59

the blindfold over my eyes. None of this jerk routine of hitting me over the head, that's for television. I get in the car. Leave the blindfold on after we get to your hideout. Mademoiselle Flanagan can tell me if she's all right.

"I give you the code word I've already arranged with Monsieur Dudley. You telephone here, give him the word, and he delivers the money. As soon as you pick it up, you fade with a Cicero Drop."

"A what?"

Colby sighed. "A Cicero Drop is simply a Healy Pickup in reverse. You drive Mademoiselle Flanagan and me, still blindfolded, to some place in the country where it'll take us an hour to walk to a telephone, and release us. I've never seen any of you, and I don't know where I've been. No strain, no *flics*. I'll bring the proof you've got the wrong woman, and I'll also bring your letter so you can burn it yourself. And one more thing. You'll have to tell me how you want the money delivered, before I go out there, so I can tell Monsieur Dudley. You got all that?"

"Yes. But we want more than thirty thousand francs."

"You won't get any more. Talk it over with your mob and call me back. And don't take all night, I haven't got much time."

"I will call you." The line went dead.

Colby replaced the instrument. Dudley was bursting with curiosity. "What'd he say, what'd you say?"

"We may be selling him," Colby replied. "But it's a long way down from a hundred thousand to six."

For Dudley's benefit, Martine repeated the gist of Colby's end of the conversation. "Everybody knows that Cheek-ago is all gangsters," she explained. "And *les gangsters américains* are the world's best." She smiled at Colby. "I loved the Healy Pickup. You've probably added a new word to *franglais*."

"Well, I always wanted to leave some monument."

"Do you think they'll go for it?"

"It's hard to guess——" he began, when the telephone rang. It hadn't taken them long to make up their minds. He picked it up, said, "Allo!" and was greeted by a burst of machine-gun French from a Parisian operator. New York was calling Madame Manning. He groaned, motioned to Dudley, and put his hand over the transmitter as he held it out.

"Cut it short," he whispered. If the kidnapers got a busy signal when they called back, the whole thing might collapse.

"Hello! Hello!" Dudley snapped. "Who? . . . Oh, Thornhill? . . . Just fine. . . ." The haunted look was back in his eyes again.

Martine leaned over. She cupped her hands and whispered in Colby's ear. "Her literary agent—driving Merriman crazy about the manuscript—calls here every other day—wants to talk to Manning. . . ."

Dudley was in front of the desk. "No, no, I wouldn't dream of interrupting her. . . . Another week at the most. . . . What? What's that?" They saw the haunted look begin to give way to one of sheer horror. "Rome? When? . . . Just a minute, somebody on the other line, I'll get rid of him—" He cupped a hand over the transmitter. "Thornhill! He's flying to Rome tonight, and he's going to stop off here to see Miss Manning!"

Well, it was interesting while it lasted, Colby thought. But this was the end. And they could kiss the six thousand dollars goodbye.

Dudley was shouting into the phone again. "Look, Thornhill, I'd think it'd be as much in your interest as it is in hers to let her finish! . . . What? . . . Of course I realize. . . ."

Martine grabbed the scratchpad and scrawled the word *F L U* across it. She held it up, gesturing.

". . . she doesn't work at night, but she does have to rest sometime!" Dudley caught sight of the scrawl. "And besides, she's got the flu."

Colby watched, fascinated. Martine had got up and was creaking her way around the desk, a middle-aged woman ravaged by grippe. Dudley broke off and stared too as she approached. She held a finger under her nose like someone trying to arrest a sneeze. She sneezed, and said, "Oh, Berribad, is thad Bister Thordhiud?" She gestured for the phone.

"Wait—here she is now," Dudley said in a faint voice. He collapsed against one of the filing cases, his face in his hands.

". . . doh, doh, id's dod the grippe. Berribad exaggerades so;

61

id's just a head code, I thig. . . . A little fever, bud dod buch, aroud a hundred and four. . . . I'b stid workig. The doctor fusses, bud. . . ."

Watching her, Colby wanted to move back to keep from catching it himself. It wasn't only the nasal voice and stuffed-up enunciation; she was ill in every line. She sneezed again.

"Oh, Berribad, would you hadd be a kleedeggs?"

Colby flipped open her handbag and passed her a handkerchief. She honked into it, and said, "Thagyou. . . . Dear Berribad's bed so dice, keepig peopud frob botherig be. . . . The book is goig very dicely, dod bore that addot̲er week . . . To Robe? . . . Oh, I wish you could stob here."

Colby was suddenly aware of an altercation somewhere below in heated and rapid-fire French, full of volleying *alors* and *vous alors!* It seemed to be drawing nearer, and he thought one of the voices was Madame Buffet's.

". . . it is a shabe," Martine went on. "It would have bed so dice to see you, but perhabs id's best. . . . Yes, I probise, right back id bed. . . . Goodbye."

She hung up, winked at Colby, and said, "He's a regular old maid about his health." Then she heard the commotion in the hall, and turned.

The rolling barrage of French was coming this way. Sandwiched between vehement protestations by Madame Buffet, a man's voice was raised in some maudlin lament that sounded like, "Bougie! I want my Bougie!" Colby stepped to the door, wondering what new crisis was about to enliven the literary scene.

The man was in the lead, plowing ahead with Madame Buffet hauling back on his coat sleeve like some terrier attached to a bear, a swarthy, tough-looking spiv with the aura of North African alleys about him in spite of the tight silk suit and pointed shoes. He was almost certainly carrying a gun in a holster under his left arm, and was weeping into a large blue handkerchief.

There was no doubt he looked and sounded drunk, but Colby felt the hair lift on his neck at the thought of that briefcase with fifty thousand francs lying on the table. He could have followed

Dudley from the bank. He came through the doorway, still towing Madame Buffet, and searched the room with as piteous a glance as was possible from a man who looked as if he would cut your throat for two dollars, or less if your shoes would fit.

The room was swept by language, most of it from Madame Buffet.

"This drunken species of camel——"

"Where's Bougie? What have you done with her?" the man sobbed, dabbing at his eyes again.

"——pushed his way in. I keep telling him there's nobody here named Bougie——" This much she had addressed to the still benumbed Dudley before remembering the futility of trying to tell him anything in French, even under optimum conditions. She swung around then and loosed the rest of the burst at Colby.

"——and if he doesn't get out we will summon the *flics*——"

Dudley was still leaning against the filing cabinets. Martine was in front of the desk. It was the man himself Colby was watching. He still looked drunk, and maybe he was, but crying into that big handkerchief was one way to keep his face hidden, and there'd been no doubt about the holster. With Madame Buffet hauling back on his coat, it had opened just enough to reveal part of the strap over his shoulder. He was inside the doorway now, with Madame Buffet to one side and slightly behind him.

"——and they can take him off in the lettuce-basket, him and——"

The man reached back with his left hand then, and lobbed her into the room ahead of him. "——his *merde* of a Bougie!" she finished more or less in mid-air as she slammed into Martine.

The right hand was stabbing into his left armpit just as Colby hit him under the ear and fell on him. They crashed to the floor on the other side of the doorway. The gun came free and slid across the rug, but the man had heaved up under him like a cat, and rolled, and they were on top of it again—or rather, Colby was on the gun and the man was on top of Colby. He was an alley-fighter's alley-fighter, fast, powerful, and dirty.

The thumbs were groping for his eyes when Colby managed

to get both feet up into his stomach and kick out. The man shot upward and back, and was on his feet directly in front of the door to the inner office when Martine emerged from it with the remains of a chair. She swung from the ankles, like a circus roustabout driving a stake. It was good, heavy, Siamese teak, and made one of the most gratifying sounds Colby had ever heard. The man straightened slightly, and looked around with an expression of gentle wonder on his face. He stepped over Colby, as though headed for the door, took two more steps, and walked into the wall. With a peaceful little sigh, he slid down it, and lay still.

The whole thing had taken only seconds. Dudley was still beside the filing cabinets, a stunned look on his face. Madame Buffet had taken refuge at the end of the desk. Colby scrambled over beside the man. He was out cold, and needed no further attention at the moment. Martine threw the remains of the chair back into the other room and picked up the gun. It was some kind of foreign automatic Colby wasn't familiar with.

"Watch it, watch it!" he called. "The safety may be off."

Martine examined it. "I'm not sure which way it goes." She pointed the muzzle at the ceiling and pulled the trigger. The report crashed back and forth, reverberating between the walls, and chunks of plaster began to rain down on Madame Buffet. Dudley buried his face in his hands again. Martine pushed the safety catch. "That way," she said, and handed the gun to Colby.

One final piece of plaster fell into Madame Buffet's hair, and the room was at rest. "*Excrément,*" she said.

"Call the cook," Colby ordered, dropping the gun in his pocket. For the moment they were, miraculously, down to only one crisis again, but he had to get the room cleared before that phone rang. "Help him drag this guy out in the alley."

"Not in there?" she asked, indicating the back room.

"No. We just get rid of him."

She started for the door, muttering. Who would ever understand Americans? A perfectly good two-hundred-franc pigeon walked in off the street and they threw him away.

"You can take storage and handling charges out of his pocket," Colby called after her. "Split with the cook."

She brightened and quickened her pace. He caught the man's shoulders, dragged him into the hall, and checked his pulse. He was all right; it would take more than a girl with a teak chair to kill him. He hurried back. Martine was dumping plaster off the two maps and putting the scratchpad back in place.

Dudley collapsed in the chair at the end of the desk. "And I could have been a pimp," he said, "or a geek in a carnival side-show——"

"Was this type in the bank when you got the money?" Colby asked. The time lag puzzled him; why had he waited so long?

"Who?" The other was still glassy-eyed, and seemed to be having trouble picking up the threads again. "Oh—no, I didn't see him." He looked at Martine.

She shook her head. "I'm sure he wasn't there."

There were grunts and mutterings in the hall as Madame Buffet and the cook began dragging the man toward the stairs.

"But what was this thing he kept saying—this Bougie business?" Dudley asked. "I thought he was looking for somebody."

"Just part of his drunk act," Colby said. "Bougie's not even a name. It's French for sparkplug."

"Or candle," Martine said.

They looked at each other. At that moment the telephone rang. Colby picked it up. "Allo."

"So you have been talking to the police! Maybe you want to get back a dead woman——!"

It was what he'd been afraid of. "Hold it," he interrupted. "And don't say cop to me. That was long-distance from Chicago. They want some action. And I've got another job——"

"What?"

"I've got to get some of our office staff up from Marseille and catch a plane to Istanbul. That man that was in the accident needs a transfusion."

"I regret your troubles, but they have nothing to do with us."

"Who said they did? I'm just trying to tell you, they want me to turn this over to Decaux. I can't stooge around here forever."

"*Decaux?* Pascal Decaux? You know *him?*"

"I've met him," Colby said indifferently. Martine was watching with fascination. Decaux was a killer, probably the deadliest hoodlum in France. "He does the odd job for us, and he can handle this pay-off. He may charge you a commission——"

"We have decided," the other broke in, almost eagerly. "Have you got a map there?"

"Of course. City, and a Michelin *Grandes Routes*."

"The Michelin. Take National Route Ten to Rambouillet——"

"Right," Colby said. He was tracing it with the pencil. Martine and Dudley watched.

"——at Rambouillet, change to Route Three-oh-six to Maintenon. Turn north there, on the route to Dreux. After four kilometers there is a road on the left, not shown——"

Colby made a mark on the map, and began writing the rest of it on the scratchpad.

"Take this road. Three kilometers ahead you will cross a small wooden bridge. Get out there and start walking in the same direction at exactly nine p.m. Your driver can return the way you came, or go ahead to one of the intersecting roads and turn left to get back onto D Twenty-six west of Maintenon."

"Check. Now, about delivering the money, so I can tell Monsieur Dudley."

"Use the same road. Tell him to keep driving straight ahead until at one of the intersecting roads he will see a wine bottle lying at the edge of the gravel. If the bottle is on the right, turn right. On the left, turn left. After the turn, he is to drive at thirty kilometers an hour straight ahead, watching the left side of the road. When he sees two wine bottles lying at the edge of it, he will throw the money out, and keep going on at the same speed. If he is followed, or stops, or if there are any police in the area, you and the girl will be killed." The line went dead.

Colby repeated the instructions to Dudley and Martine. She smiled admiringly. "I think it was Decaux that swung it," she said. "That was a nice touch."

"I thought it might throw a little scare into 'em, even if it did mean stooping to the truth. I have met him, I interviewed him once." He went on. "There was nothing said about more money, but they may be saving that till I get out there. They'll have two of us then, and a bluff can work both ways. Except that if only thirty thousand francs was drawn out of the bank, it means sweating it out for another twenty-four hours, till tomorrow night. So it gets easier and easier to settle for the thirty thousand and run."

"The old pressure routine," Martine said. Then she went on soberly, "But there's still no guarantee they won't kill you both after they get it."

"There never is. It just depends on how well we've sold them we're not going to the police. Is there a safe here?"

"Yes," Dudley replied. "In that back room."

"Put the money in there. And make sure all the outside doors are locked, so that joker can't get back in. Martine will take the gun in the car, both trips. She'll drop me, and then come back here. When they call, you answer. The code word is 'bingo.' Put thirty thousand francs in the briefcase, all the small bills and the rest in hundreds. You and Martine deliver it, and then come back here and wait for us to call. If we do, your troubles are over. If we don't, ours are."

The car was a Jaguar, an XKE roadster, and Martine drove it in the French manner, with the hell-for-leather *élan* of the cavalry charge at Agincourt, and the same fine contempt for consequences. Traffic was heavy until they were out of the city, calling mostly for great agility and a certain fluency in verbal exchange with other drivers, but presently the spaces between cars began to lengthen and there was more scope for California roulette. At least, Colby thought, it took his mind off tonight; there didn't seem to be any great chance he'd live to see it.

"It's just the other side of Rambouillet," he reminded her. "Not in the Pyrenees."

"I thought if we had time we'd have dinner somewhere," she said, knifing back into line in front of an oncoming truck with inches to spare.

They stopped at an *auberge* in Rambouillet. While they were sipping their *apéritifs*, she asked, "Why *bougie?*"

"I don't get it either. But he was after the money—he must have been."

68

"I suppose." She frowned. "But—candle—Kendall."

"Just a coincidence. You don't translate names. And how would she know a thug like that?"

Martine smiled. "I don't know. But with Flanagan, don't bet n anything."

In one of his pockets Colby had a folded dust jacket from *These Tormented* by Sabine Manning, and Kendall Flanagan's passport. He took out the latter and opened it. A knockout, he thought, even in a passport photo. "What kind of girl is she?"

"Out of a Norse myth, by Rabelais," Martine said. "A silver blonde, six feet tall and around one hundred and sixty pounds, and as unbuttoned as the second day of a wake."

"*Six feet?*"

"It's right there. Look."

Colby glanced at the data on the front page. She was right. *Height: 6 – 0.* He whistled. *Birthplace: Wyoming. Aug. 18, 1937.*

"But it's all girl," Martine went on, "and in the right places. She has what novelists used to call an appetite for living. Her theory is we're all double-parked, and tomorrow may be called off on account of rain. She's the last person you'd ever expect to be writing that syrupy drivel for TV commercials, but as she says, she discovered she had a knack for it, it pays better than trying to teach English to high-school kids, and she had to give up modeling because bearskin rugs made her break out with hives.

"Actually, she can imitate any style of writing, and this stuff of Manning's was a cinch for her. She did a page of it in Faulkner one day, just to bug Merriman, and it was perfect. She could write as fast as Sanborn, too, but she's just not overwhelmed with the seriousness of it all. The reason he got ahead of her is he slept nights.

"Sometimes she wouldn't get home till ten a.m., long after he'd gone to work. For breakfast she'd have a split of champagne, six cups of coffee, and three or four eggs, and then sit down at the typewriter and start banging away. Vitality galore."

"I can see how she and Dudley might get on each other's nerves," Colby said.

"Oh, she never paid any attention to him. She just laughed at him or brushed him off like a gnat—except that morning they had the argument, I mean. She was apparently upset about something, and when he started complaining about her late hours, she blew up and told him off."

"And that was the day she was kidnaped."

"Yes. Nobody saw her leave, but apparently it was in the evening. They must have picked her up in front of the house."

Colby nodded, and turned his attention to the photograph of Sabine Manning on the back of the book jacket. It was the usual gussied-up job of the glamour photographer, softened and diaphanous and full of subtly hinted mystery, but no amount of technique could entirely cover up the spinsterish aspect of its small, prim mouth, the lost and defeated wallflower face, and its drab topping of undistinguished hair that was probably somewhere between brindle and dried-thistle brown.

"What's she like?" he asked Martine.

"It's not a kind thing to say," she replied with some reluctance, "but mousy is the word you have to use. She's just one of those people that nothing ever happens to, that nobody ever sees——"

"No charisma."

"Worse. The girl at the cocktail party hiding in a corner with an empty glass pretending to be interested in book titles on a shelf. I thought when Roberto shook her up she was going to live a little, but maybe it was too late."

"She might have found another boyfriend. I mean, if Roberto left her."

"It's possible, I suppose. But she's so—so ineffectual, the poor dear. Actually, we don't even *know* she went away with Roberto in the first place; we just assumed she did. That postcard from Samos sounded so ecstatic . . . I don't know, it baffles me."

It was a narrow gravel road running between hedges. "Two kilometers," Colby said.

He glanced at his watch in the glow of the instrument panel. Six minutes to nine. Just after making the turn they'd passed a farmhouse showing lights, but he could see no more ahead. It was lonely enough. A rabbit bolted across the road ahead of them. Then he picked up the wooden bridge.

"Three kilometers on the nose," he said, as they rolled across it and stopped. "This is the place."

"I'll go on and turn left to get back to the highway." She was silent for a moment and then shivered slightly, and said, "I almost wish we hadn't got mixed up in this. I'm scared, Colby."

"So am I," he said. He turned. Faint starlight shone in her eyes and he was conscious of the subtle hint of perfume. Then she was in his arms and he was kissing her to the accompaniment of fireworks and violins.

"You're beautiful," he said. "Damn it to hell——"

"Mmmmmmm—what?"

"The bucket seat. Nobody but an automobile manufacturer——"

"Well, the pills can't do it all."

"Have you ever been to Rhodes?"

"Uuuuummmmmm-uuuuummmmm."

"What?"

"No," she said.

"It's wonderful there——"

"That joke's older than both of us."

"I didn't mean the joke. Rhodes. Bougainvillea, wine-dark sea, roses, music. Tomorrow we'll have six thousand dollars——"

"You do the most exciting audit. Or is it a travelogue?"

"Will you?"

"I think I might be persuaded. Let you know tomorrow?"

"All right." He broke it up, reluctant to let her go, said "Geronimo," and stepped out. She blew him a kiss. The taillights of the Jaguar disappeared down the road.

He lighted a cigarette, waited a minute until his eyes had adjusted to the darkness, and began walking slowly ahead along the left side of the road, his mind still swamped and overrun with the prospect of this intoxicating girl against the perfect background of Rhodes. It was going to be worth getting involved in Dudley's madhouse.

It was a beautiful night, clear, but moonless, and crisp with autumn without being cold. He wore only the tweed suit, having left the topcoat at the house. The shadowy masses of the hedges continued, closing him in on both sides. In less than ten minutes the headlights showed behind him. In spite of himself, he felt his nerves begin to tighten.

The car came on, slowed, and went past. He recognized the distinctive, carapace silhouette of a Citroën. After it had gone out of sight, he remembered the lipstick, and scrubbed at his lips with a handkerchief. It was supposed to be Dudley who'd dropped him, and the fewer things he had to explain the better. His shoes made a crunching sound on the gravel. Now the car was coming back.

The headlights were on high beam, blinding him. He felt for the edge of the gravel with his feet to give it room to go past if it were the wrong one. But it was already slowing. It came to a stop less than twenty feet away. He turned his back and put his hands on top of his head.

Footsteps sounded in the gravel, two sets of them, and came up behind him. He felt the hair lift on his neck. A voice growled, "If the *salaud* twitches a muscle, shoot him!"

Naturally theatrical, he wondered, or just trying to impress the *gangstair américain*? Or maybe they hadn't bought a word of it; it was possible they didn't read the *Série Noire*. Hands patted him under the arms, on the pockets, and ran down his trouser legs.

"Nothing," another voice said.

A dark cloth was placed over his eyes and knotted behind his head. Then there was the tearing sound of tape being unrolled as the man wound it around and around his head, over the blindfold and into his hair. A hand guided him back to the car. He groped, found the open rear door. He got in.

"Kneel," the voice said. He crouched on his knees, his face on his arms atop the seat. He heard the others get in, in front, and the door closed. Something cold and hard nudged the back of his head, and the voice said, "No tricks. Brains are hard to clean off upholstery."

He had a fine flair for drama, Colby thought; he was feeling less nervous now. It was impossible to tell which of them he'd talked to—the French telephone is seldom a high-fidelity instrument. The gun muzzle left his head, but he knew it was still pointed at him. The car lunged forward with the sound of scattered gravel. It was a Citroën, all right; he recognized the exaggerated vertical movement of its shock-absorbers.

The first turn was to the left, which meant they were going away from Maintenon, but after that he paid no attention. It would be elementary, even for a child, to make an unnecessary number of them, going in a twisting, roundabout route, in order to confuse him. He lost track of time. It could have been thirty minutes later, or forty-five, when they made a sharp turn, bounced over a rough road for some hundred meters, made two turns in quick succession, and stopped. Doors opened.

"Descend," one of the voices said.

He climbed out, his knees cramped from kneeling on the floor. He was conscious of the ubiquitous odor of rotting manure of all continental farms, and heard a horse kick his stall. He was in a barnyard.

A hand took his arm, and he felt the gun in his back. After three or four steps he felt concrete or flagstone under his feet, and then a mat. He wiped his shoes. One of them brushed something that moved with a wooden clatter. Probably a pair of sabots. A door clicked open, and he was pushed into a room with a bare wooden floor. No light at all penetrated the blindfold, but he could feel the warmth of a stove nearby, and smell coffee and the residual odors of cooking.

The whole ride had been in silence, but this was now swept away with the suddenness of a collapsing dike. "*Alors!* Another *pensionnaire!*" It was a female voice, young, assertive, and charged with accumulated grievance. "Maybe we will get in the *Guide Michelin*, with a star, and crossed manure forks——"

"*Écoute——!*"

"Another one to cook for and wash dishes for, when I'm not shoveling food down that bottomless pit of a woman, or scrubbing floors, or milking your Uncle Anatole's excrement of a cow——"

"Quiet!" one of the men shouted. "This one lays the golden egg."

"Hah! Like your Uncle Anatole's imbecile of a horse lays the golden egg in a basket of laundry——"

"*Tais toi,* Gabrielle! One should never put things down near a horse——"

D'accord! Not near the horse of Uncle Anatole. Or the cow of Uncle Anatole, or the chickens, or the sheep, or anything else in this paradise where constipation was only a rumor. If she ever saw a piece of pavement again. . . .

Colby stood in silence while language played around his head. Then somebody caught him by the arm and he was pushed into a chair. He could feel a table in front of him. "Listen!" a voice shouted, as a fist banged the table, causing dishes to rattle. "This one says she is not Mademoiselle Manning. Let us examine his so-called proof!"

"In my right-hand coat pocket," Colby said.

"Aha! He does not speak with the accent of Cheek-ago!"

"What do you know of the accent of Cheek-ago? You have heard it in films, with French actors——"

"*Alors!* So Oomfrey Bogarr is a French actor——"

"It is never the voice of Oomfrey Bogarr!"

"To hell with the accent of this one! Let us see the proof."

A hand dug into his pocket and brought out the folded dust jacket and Kendall Flanagan's passport.

"*Voilà!* It is the passport of ours."

"And the faces are not the same."

"Writers put other names on their books, why not other faces?"

"*Regard!* If you had the face of ours, would you put the face of that one on your book?"

"So! You too!" It was the girl's voice. "Maybe *I* should keep the key to her room."

"I am only stating what anyone can see——"

"You are as sickening as Jean-Jacques. You would need the equipment of *alpinisme*. I see you, roped together, mounting the north wall of this blonde Alp——"

"Quiet! We must decide."

"What is there to decide? Truly, she is not Mademoiselle Manning. We take the money and we go."

"But thirty thousand francs——"

All the voices erupted at once, but it was the girl's Colby was following. She was full up to here with Uncle Anatole's farm. This was the Paris she'd been promised? The *discothèques*, the Moulin Rouge, the Champs Élysées, champagne? For five days she'd been up to her knees in *fumier*, taking care of an idiot of a cow, and cooking food and opening bottles of wine for the unbelievable appetite of this unbelievable species of woman who was the wrong woman to begin with. And besides, Uncle Anatole might return tomorrow——

She was immediately pounced upon and silenced, but Colby had caught it. He was going to win; they had to settle tonight. He gave no sign he'd heard, but said curtly, "Nobody gets anything until I've talked to Mademoiselle Flanagan."

"You shall talk to her."

"Good. Give me back the passport. And your letter is in my left-hand pocket."

The passport was placed in his hand. He returned it to his pocket. Someone else removed the letter.

"What a species of imbecility, in your own handwriting," the

75

girl's voice said. "It's a good thing you have an American *gang-stair* to tell you how to conduct an affair of this sort."

"Come," one of the voices said. He stood up, and was turned, marched forward, and turned again. He thought they were going down a hallway. They stopped. He heard a key being inserted in a lock, and had an impression of a door opening.

"She will tell you she is all right," the man said. It was the one called Jean-Jacques. Then he warned, "No English."

"Mademoiselle Flanagan?" Colby asked, addressing the blackness directly ahead of him.

"Yes. Who are you?" There was no fear in the voice, which seemed to be coming from the far side of a room. It was pure American French; they weren't running in a ringer on him.

"Duke Colby, from Chicago," he said. "I work for Carl. Trouble-shooter, enforcer—like that." He wasn't sure how much of this she could understand, but it was for the others anyway. "I flew in today to see if I could cool this thing before it got loused up with cops or newspapers."

"How is Carl?"

"Chewing nails, you know him. He wanted to move in with a bunch of muscle, but I talked him out of it. Bad for business. You're okay, then?"

"No complaints."

"That's all I wanted to know. Dudley's just waiting for word from me to deliver the payoff. I'll see you."

The key turned in the lock again. "Now, are you satisfied?" Jean-Jacques asked.

"Yes," he said. "Call the same number. When Monsieur Dudley answers, say only one word. Bingo."

"*Beengo.*"

"That's it. He'll deliver the money as soon as he can get there."

"*Beengo.* Remember it well, Rémy."

He was marched back along the hallway a few steps and apparently into another room. His hands were tied behind him, and he was pushed backward onto a bed. "We are being robbed," Jean-Jacques complained bitterly. "Thirty thousand francs—hah! But what can one do? We will drop you with the Cicero."

They went out. He could hear them in the kitchen, still arguing, still addressing each other by name. In a few minutes a door slammed and there was silence except for an occasional banging of pots and pans by Gabrielle. They had gone to phone Dudley. He shook his head. In a deal like this, give him professionals every time; these *blousons noirs* were careless and reckless enough to freeze his blood except that he'd been lucky enough to sell them the Chicago story.

In the twenty minutes he'd been here he'd learned enough about them for the police to locate the farm in an hour, with nothing but a copy of the tax rolls and the telephone numbers of the local *gendarmeries*. It was owned by a man named Anatole, who'd been away somewhere on a trip and who had a nephew named Jean-Jacques. Jean-Jacques had a friend named Rémy, whose girl friend was called Gabrielle. They'd pick them up in an afternoon. Well, it didn't matter; he'd convinced them nobody was going to the police.

With his hands bound behind him, there was no way to get comfortable in bed. After awhile he sat up on the side of it, wishing he had a cigarette. The bonds weren't tight enough to cut off circulation, and he could probably have worked his way out of them if he'd tried, but it would be stupid. He would accomplish nothing except to antagonize them, which was the last thing he wanted now that success was in sight.

There was nothing to do but wait, as he had a thousand times in the Army. He had no idea how many hours later it was when he heard the kitchen door fly open and then the sound of their voices, all three talking at once. He started to grin, but it faded. Something had changed. He leaned forward, listening intently. He could make out only a word now and then, but there was some quality in the voices that hadn't been there before. A chill moved slowly up his spine as he began to place it. It was panic.

What could have gone wrong? They must have the money by now, and certainly there couldn't have been any police in the area. But several times he heard the word among the shouts and violent recriminations. They were scared to death, and blaming

77

each other. The flap went on for what could have been ten minutes, and then the key turned in his door.

"You. Get up." It was Jean-Jacques' voice, and there was an unnecessary toughness in it again, as there had been when they'd picked him up. There was no doubt he was scared.

Colby stood up. "The money was delivered?"

"Yes. We have it."

"And there were no police, just as I promised?"

"We saw none."

"So you're going to release us?"

"Of course we're going to release you, *salaud*! What do you think, we want to adopt you?"

He's lying, Colby thought. For some reason now they think they have to kill us, and they're trying to work themselves up to it. But what had happened?

He was marched along the hallway. They were apparently back in the kitchen, judging from the odors, though he could no longer feel any warmth from the stove. He could hear the voices of Rémy and Gabrielle somewhere behind him.

"How about untying my hands?" Colby asked.

"Shut up! We will untie your hands when we get there." Then, apparently to the others, "Her handbag, everything! Be sure nothing is left."

He heard a new sound, the clicking of high heels along the hall. Gabrielle hadn't worn them, so they were bringing Kendall Flanagan. He was marched ahead, heard the door open, and they were outside in the barnyard. "Her first," Jean-Jacques ordered. "Now this one." He was pushed forward. A hand forced his head down. Getting in was awkward with his hands tied, and he fell over against Kendall. He was hauled into the position he'd been in before, kneeling with his face down on the seat. Kendall was on his right. "Stay down!" a voice commanded. He heard the three of them get in the front seat. The car shot backward, swung, and surged ahead. Almost immediately there was an explosive curse in French and it slammed to a stop. What now?

One of the front doors opened and he heard running footsteps going away. In a moment they came back. The trunk opened, and something was thrown in it, something that landed with a metallic clang. He froze. A shovel? No, he told himself, fighting panic, it could have been something else. The car lunged ahead again. They bounced and jolted their way to the road, and made a left turn with tires squealing as they came onto the pavement.

"Something's bugged them," Kendall said next to his ear.

"Silence!" a voice shouted from in front. "No English."

"How about French, then?" She said several words Colby wouldn't have thought she'd know. But then she'd been here five days.

"Shut up, or I will shoot!"

She fell silent. Colby could hear the three of them arguing in violent whispers in the front seat. It was ominous, and he was conscious of a cold and empty feeling in his stomach. He could make out only an occasional word, but heard police several times.

"What's the matter with you?" he asked. "Don't you know by now we're not going to the police?"

"They're not going to the police, he says—hah!" It was the girl.

"Shut up!" Jean-Jacques shouted. "Everybody talks too much!"

Colby felt his heart leap then. Kendall's hands weren't tied. One of them had moved over and was resting on his. She'd probably been tied to the bed and they'd merely released her in their hurry. The fingers moved, exploring the turns of rope around his wrists. She began to tug at the knot.

She might be able to do it, he thought, hardly daring to hope. His hands were directly below and behind the three of them in the front seat, and unless one turned all the way around and looked down they might not see it. Also, it was still dark. Or should be; he didn't think it could be dawn yet.

They were traveling at high speed, their tires screaming on the turns. He felt the ropes give a little, but dreaded from one minute to the next he'd hear the shout of discovery and the impact of a gun barrel on her head or arm. The warfare of impassioned whispers was still going on in the front seat. He could catch a word or phrase now and then. "... *you and your stupid ideas! ... everything wrong ... talk too much. ...*" Then one that spread the chill between his shoulder blades. ". . . *no, this was your idea, you do it!*"

The ropes slipped then and gave way. His hands were free.

"Hit the dirt," Kendall said. Then his ears were assaulted by a scream that years later would still come back and echo along his nerves.

He was swinging his upper body toward the floor when the car seemed to take off like a jet at the end of a runway. It dipped, and then went up, and there was a sound like the snapping of violin strings. Just as he was beginning to think it was airborne for good, it crashed down, still upright, with a cannonading of exploded tires, and plowed into something he could only assume was a solid wall of water. There was a great *wh-o-o-o-shing* sound like a giant exhalation of breath, accompanied by violent deceleration that plastered him against the back of the seat in front of him. It lurched then, and began to roll. It went all the way over once, with a crashing and rending of metal and a snapping off of burst-open doors, came upright, and then over again, almost gently this time and with a strange, feltlike absence of sound, as though it had found a bed to climb into to die.

His eardrums must have ruptured, Colby thought. No, he could still hear the engine. Blindfolded, and after having been in total darkness for hours and then whirled in this centrifuge, he had no idea where he was or which way was up. He was groggy and bruised, but nothing seemed to be broken. He could move his arms and legs. One of his hands brushed the upholstery of the seat, directly over his head.

There was an eruption of outcries in French, and the car began to rock gently from side to side. He could smell gasoline, and could hear the engine still purring, while the whole thing seemed to quiver with a strange, jellylike vibration. He threw his hands about again, seeking a way out before it burst into flames, and where the door had been he could feel straw. There were probably a number of ways you could explain that, he thought. Say, for example, the car was upside down on top of a haystack.

He heard a succession of dry, swishing sounds nearby, and

more curses in French. But he had to locate Kendall and get them out before it caught fire. The smell of gasoline was growing stronger. He swung his arms, but they encountered nothing except the seat over his head and the back of the front one. She was gone. He groped for the door again. The opening wasn't completely filled with straw. At the top, near the floor of the car, there was a space where his hand met nothing. He began to push his way out, like a surfacing mole. A hand caught his arm and hauled. He was out, lying in more straw.

"We may have set a new record for making it to the hay," Kendall said. The hand let go his arm, there was another rustling, plunging sound, and he was alone.

He sat up, tearing at the blindfold, and then the straw gave way under him and he was sliding backward down a gentle incline. The blindfold tore off just as he hit bottom and came to rest, his head and shoulders on the ground and his feet still up on the slope above him.

He was looking straight up at the Citroën. It lay on its back atop the haystack, slanting down a little forward, the engine still humming while its hind wheels turned futilely in the air and its headlights searched the darkness like great anguished eyes imploring help. It looked, Colby thought, as though it had climbed out onto the beach to lay its eggs and somebody had flipped it over on its back to make soup out of it.

He heard an impact of some kind, followed by a grunt. He turned then, and saw Kendall Flanagan for the first time.

It was a sight that would be stamped into his memory forever with the perfection of detail and sharpness of definition of something caught on high-speed film with a strobe light, and while he learned later this was not an uncommon experience among men on whom she burst in full glory this suddenly and without any preparation at all, there was the fact that in his case she was clothed. In another instance, of which he heard later, she was as naked as a radish. The searing effect of this, and its potentiality for erasing even the memory of all previous visual experience, was something on which the mind could only speculate.

All the judo experts he ever told about it afterward were unanimous in the opinion it was impossible; given the acceleration of falling bodies and the time necessary to fit the shoulder into the socket under the arm, bend forward, and throw, she simply couldn't have had both of them in the air at once, but he knew what he saw. Maybe he didn't know judo, but they didn't know Kendall Flanagan.

She was directly in the beam of the headlights like an illuminated tableau of some Old Testament miracle, six feet and one hundred and sixty pounds of stacked and silvery blonde in a black cocktail dress, silver high-heeled slippers, and a rope of pearls, while out in front of her near the end of his trajectory Jean-Jacques/Rémy was still airborne a hundredth of a second before landing on the back of his neck, and the leather-jacketed form of Rémy/Jean-Jacques was just coming off her shoulder, already separated and beginning to wheel upward and out into the same flight pattern.

The first landed with a tooth-rattling thud and lay still. Almost instantaneously the other crashed down beside him in an identical position, tried once to get up, thought better of it, and lay back. She straightened her dress.

"If you need any help," Colby said, "I can whip the girl."

"Oh, she's over there." Kendall turned and pointed behind her. In the edge of the headlight beam, the girl was just sitting up. Kendall looked around at the devastation to see if anybody was in the mood for seconds, flashed a joyous smile in Colby's direction, and suggested, "Maybe we'd better move out. That gun is still around here somewhere."

She turned and climbed up the haystack. Thinking she might be going to throw the car down, Colby scrambled to his feet to get out of the way. She knelt beside it and groped around inside. "Catch," she said, and Dudley's briefcase sailed out toward him. He caught it, and at the same moment she said, "Wheeeeel" and disappeared down the other side.

Colby ran around, but she had only slid down. She was sitting up, tugging her skirt and slip down from under her arms. She stood up, carrying her handbag, took a couple of steps, and halted with a gurgle of amusement. "Hold this a minute," she asked, passing Colby the purse, and began to grope under her skirt. "Hay in my pants," she said. "Man bites dog."

The girl was shouting imprecations in French behind them now, urging Jean-Jacques and Rémy on to the pursuit. This was apparently encountering some lack of enthusiasm, for she began crying out for somebody to find the gun. Colby and Kendall hurried on. His eyes were adjusting to the darkness again, and directly ahead he could see an exploded haystack that looked as though somebody had lobbed a mortar shell into it.

This was what they'd hit that had slowed them down. Just beyond it were the burst strands of a wire fence, and then the road. It made a sweeping turn here, coming toward the field and its haystacks and then going off at almost right angles.

"What did you do to him?" Colby asked, as they ran across the ditch and up onto the pavement.

"When I screamed," Kendall replied, "I put my blindfold over his eyes."

Going into a turn at a hundred kilometers an hour, Colby thought; it would have an unsettling effect on a driver. If word ever got around, she should be as unlikely a prospect for future kidnapings as Red Chief.

The gun barked behind them then, and something snicked through the branches of a tree on the other side of the road. They could hear sounds of pursuit, and turned right, running along the pavement. Kendall stopped, yanked off the high-heeled slippers, and sprinted on. Colby took the purse from her, carrying the briefcase in his other hand. There was enough starlight for the others to see them in the open like this, but another fifty yards ahead on the left was a dark line of timber. They plunged into it, groped their way on for a few more yards, and crouched down in a clump of evergreens. They could hear the pounding of footsteps along the pavement, and shouts, and one of the men made a foray into the timber, crashing through the underbrush less than twenty yards away.

The tumult went on down the road, but a few minutes later the three of them were back again, still arguing violently and blaming each other. The voices died away in the direction of the car.

"I think they intended to kill us," Kendall said. "Don't you?"

"Yes," he said. It still baffled him. "Something queered it when they went to pick up the money."

"Do you suppose it *is* money? Dudley would rather open a vein than part with ten francs."

"Martine wouldn't have stood for anything like that," he said. "Besides, he had to get you back to finish the book." He unzipped the briefcase and flicked on his cigarette lighter, shielding the flame with his body. It was filled with bundles of francs—tens, fifties, and hundreds, just as Dudley had brought it from the bank.

"It beats me," he said. He was overcome with yearning for a cigarette, and they were sufficiently screened by the dense underbrush. He took out the pack. "Smoke?"

"I'd love one. Thanks."

Over the flame of the lighter he had a brief glimpse of a very lovely face and amused and utterly reckless gray eyes. "You're a friend of Martine's then?" she asked. "I thought you might be, from that Cosa Nostra routine."

"I met her a couple of days ago." Was it only two days? It didn't seem possible. "Dudley hired us to get you back."

"How is Sunny Jim? Ilium is doomed? There's no hope for the whooping crane?"

Colby grinned. "He just doesn't trust the situation. Some OB man conned him into being born before he could check with his lawyer."

There was continued silence from the direction of the road. When they had ground out their cigarettes, they eased back to it. The farther they were from the area by daybreak, the better. There was no sign of the others. They started walking, Kendall still carrying her shoes. A few hundred yards ahead they went around another turn and there was still no sound of pursuit. A half-hour later it was growing light in the east. They came to an intersection with another road. Paris was one hundred and ten

kilometers to the right, a sign said, and the next village was St.-
Médard-au-bout-de-la-colline, fourteen kilometers.

Two or three cars went past, but refused to stop. Then, just
as it was full light, Colby managed to flag down a farmer in a
battered old truck loaded with sheep. They'd had an accident,
he explained, and would like a lift to St.-Médard. There wasn't
room for both of them in the cab, so Colby helped her in beside
the driver and climbed in back among the sheep. The old truck
rumbled, and crawled ahead. After it had gone about a mile, it
lurched suddenly and almost ran off the road. This puzzled him
until a shredded pair of nylons flew out the window and sailed
past. He grinned.

The sun came up. It was a crisp, exhilarating morning with air
like champagne. He felt wonderful. It was in the bag now; it had
been a highly profitable night, and successful beyond all ex-
pectation. Maybe they should brace Dudley for a bonus, to be
split with Kendall, for having recovered the thirty thousand
francs. In another hour or two he'd see Martine again, and if his
luck continued to hold maybe by this afternoon they'd be wing-
ing their way toward Rhodes, that island whose specifications
might have been drawn up by a man with a beautiful girl on his
mind and plenty of experience in using terrain. He hummed a
few bars of "Oh, What a Beautiful Morning," and grinned at his
companions, but they merely stared back at him with the vast
apathy of sheep toward all phenomena not overtly menacing or
recognizably edible. He lighted a cigarette and was content.

St.-Médard-au-bout-de-la-colline was a small farming village
of three or four streets lying athwart the road with a church
steeple at the back of it, looking quaint and peaceful in the early
rays of the sun. The farmer stopped at the intersection of its
principal street. Colby helped her down, thanked him, and passed
him ten francs. He tipped his cap to Kendall, looked at her once
more with disbelief, and drove on. A man coming along the sidewalk craned his neck, and narrowly missed walking into a light
standard.

Besides jettisoning the ruined nylons, she had combed her hair,
which was like burnished silver springs, and repaired her make-up

during the drive. Aside from a few wrinkles in the black dress, she could be just starting out for an evening in Paris, and he was conscious of his own stubble of beard and the wisps of hay clinging to the tweed.

She grinned. "I don't know about you, but I'm ready to eat anything that doesn't attack me first."

He glanced around. It didn't appear too promising, at this time of day. Directly across from them a *boulangerie* was in business, and up in the next block a newspaper kiosk and a small café, but if there were a restaurant at all it wouldn't be open till time for lunch. But there should be a telephone in the café where he could call Martine. They walked up and crossed the street. A man going past on some kind of rubber-tired farm machine turned to stare at Kendall. Colby visualized her crossing a street in Rome during an hour of peak traffic; the carnage would be staggering.

There were no tables set up on the sidewalk yet, but eight or ten inside, and a small bar with beer taps and an espresso coffee machine. Besides the *patron* behind the bar and one waiter, there were half a dozen customers, mostly in farm clothing or workers' blue denim, some of them reading the Paris newspapers. Papers were lowered and necks craned as they came in. One man, arrested in the act of raising a glass of beer to his lips, seemed in some danger of having his eyes drop in it, Colby thought, if he were to move his head suddenly.

It puzzled him; even as big and beautiful as she was, they were overdoing it for Frenchmen. Italians, maybe, but—well, this wasn't Paris, by any means. He glanced toward the bar. There was a telephone, but he'd have to wait. The *patron* had just picked it up himself. The waiter came over. He seemed dazed too.

Kendall smiled at him and said in fair French, "A bottle of champagne, four cups of coffee, some bacon, and—hmmmm—six eggs, and a plate of croissants." Even if all this were obtainable, which was unlikely, Colby wondered if she thought they could eat that much. She turned to him. "And what'll you have?"

Visibly shaken—whether by the size of the order or the size of the girl, Colby wasn't sure—the waiter started to explain it was only a café. They had no facilities for cooking champagne—that is, eggs.

"Oh," she said, disappointed. "Then bring us some ham sandwiches."

"But of course, Mademoiselle. How many?"

"Just keep bringing them till we tell you to stop."

It would take some time to chill the breasts—a thousand pardons, the champagne.

She interrupted with another smile and a wave of the hand. Bring up a bottle from the cellar; it would be cold enough. She appealed to Colby. "Impress it on him he'd better get some food on the table before he goes the way of Dr. Millmoss. Tell him I'm pregnant. Anything."

Colby grinned and said the young lady was famished. The waiter departed. She picked up the briefcase and unzipped it. "Breakfast will be on that great, open-handed patron of the arts, Lorenzo the Magnificent Dudley—hey, what is it?" She snapped her fingers. "Colby, dear, look at me."

"I am," Colby said. He was staring past her, directly over her shoulder, with a sensation like the prickling of icy needles between his shoulder blades. A man had just sat down at the next table with a newspaper and started to open it. It was *France-soir*, and covering a good quarter of the front page was a picture of Kendall Flanagan. Beside it, black headlines leaped out at him:

DID BOUGIE KILL PEPE?
WHO IS THIS RAVISHING BOUGIE?

He tried to point. He couldn't seem to move, or say anything. All he could think of was that the *patron* had already called the police. Five minutes ago.

She turned and looked. "My God!" Her elbow knocked over the briefcase, and several packets of one-hundred-franc notes spilled out on the table just as the waiter arrived with the champagne. He stopped, rooted, his mouth hanging open. Then Colby's gears meshed at last. He began scooping up the bundles of francs and cramming them back into the briefcase. Stripping a note from the last one, he threw it on the table, zipped the briefcase, and they headed for the entrance just as the gendarme trotted in.

"One moment, Mademoiselle!" he said, and made what was probably the greatest mistake of his career up to that time. He put out a hand. Colby groaned.

He went up, wheeling, came off the shoulder, and headed rearward in a spectacular flash of blue. In some corner of his mind not completely numb with horror, Colby noted that she didn't seem to be getting quite the distance she had earlier in the morning. It might have been because he was a bigger man, mature and solid and heavier all around, and perhaps a little out of balance for perfect flight trim with the gun attached to one side of his belt, but more likely it was simply because she hadn't had breakfast. He landed on a table among some coffee cups, a glass of beer, and a bottle of Evian. The table, skidding backward as it collapsed, slammed into another at which two men were sharing a *demi* of beaujolais. They all went to the floor together.

Colby was never sure afterward whether he brushed the waiter in transit, or whether the latter, simply having had it for the morning, merely dropped it, but at any rate the bottle of champagne hit the floor and exploded behind them just as they shot out the entrance. Champagne not properly chilled is brusque and ill-mannered and clamorous in its release.

They wheeled to the right. It didn't seem to make any difference, Colby thought, since they had nowhere to go except to jail, but the corner was nearer this way. They shot around it. She was having difficulty with the high heels, but two kicks sent the silver slippers out into the street, and she came abreast of him again.

"The next time I go out for an evening in Paris," she panted, "I'll wear track shoes."

They were nearly up to the next corner before the first wave of pursuers surged around the one behind them, but there was no hope whatever of escape, not in a place this size. Then he became aware of a sound somewhere ahead of them, an idling motorcycle engine. They hit the corner then, and he saw it, a big, powerful-looking machine some twenty feet off to the right, standing in front of a tobacco shop. The owner was apparently inside.

"Get aboard!" he shouted, and lunged for the seat. He hadn't ridden a motorcycle since he was nineteen, and wasn't familiar with the shift of this one, but by the time she had jumped onto the seat behind him and clasped him around the middle he had it in motion. He gunned it straight ahead. There was a shout behind them, and she made a sound he thought was a gurgle of laughter.

He turned right at the corner, and gunned it again. As they sped across the street the café was on, he shot a glance toward it. Twenty or thirty people were gathered in front, shouting and gesturing. At the next corner he turned right once more, and then left, and they were on the road out of town, the way they had come in. He had the handle of the briefcase clamped against one of the handlebars, and her purse was pressed into his stomach.

As they roared out of the turn and began to pick up speed along the road, she chuckled again just back of his ear, and said, "He was one furious gendarme."

A certain amount of pique might be understandable, Colby thought. "Well, you threw him ten feet into somebody's breakfast."

"No, not that one. The one you stole the motorcycle from."

Oh, good God! "A gendarme? You're sure?"

"Of course. He had a uniform and a gun. He was going to shoot, until he saw I was a girl. I think the French police are sweet."

He shuddered. "They can also get rougher than cobs."

It was difficult to talk through the roar of the engine and the wind whipping past their faces. They hit one hundred and twenty kilometers an hour and leveled off. He shot a glance behind them, and groaned. Not that there was any pursuit in sight yet. It was just that St.-Médard-au-bout-de-la-colline, with its church steeple in back of it, looked so quaint and peaceful in the early rays of the sun.

There had to be an answer, he told himself, but he didn't know what it was. They had no chance whatever of reaching Paris on this motorcycle; in another ten minutes all the police in this end of France would be looking for them. They couldn't go into a village to phone Martine to come after them, for the same reason. And even aside from the motorcycle, Kendall couldn't appear anywhere. There might be three or four people in France who wouldn't know de Gaulle if they saw him, but she was a celebrity.

In a few minutes they were back at the intersection. The road to the left was the one that went past the wrecked Citroën. They had to avoid that; there might be police there now. According to the sign, the next village straight ahead was sixteen kilometers. They were going away from Paris, but that seemed the best bet. An idea was beginning to occur to him. Their only hope was to get off the road and hole up within the next few minutes, before going through any villages. And he had to find a farmhouse with a telephone.

They roared on. Four or five kilometers ahead, he saw just the place. It was a prosperous-looking farm with a good-sized house set back from the road, and he could see the telephone line going in. There was no one in sight as they went past. Just beyond it the road went around a curve and down a gentle grade. At the bottom was an old stone bridge over a stream bordered with willows. There were no cars in sight and he could see no one in the fields. He cut the throttle and began to ride it down, and they screeched to a stop just at the end of the bridge. A footpath led off along the edge of the willows to the right.

She had already hopped off. He killed the engine, handed her the briefcase, and ran the machine off into the path. When they were twenty or thirty yards from the road, he wheeled and pushed it in among the willows. They were yellow with autumn, but still in full leaf. They came out onto the bank of the meandering little stream, running clear over its bed of rocks. There was a small glade here, completely hidden from the road. He propped the machine up and leaned against it, full of bitter hopelessness at the thought of Martine and Rhodes.

Kendall came up behind him, mincing over the stones on her

bare feet, and smiled with admiration. "Nice work, Colby. What do we do now?"

"Five years would be a good guess. Assaulting an officer, resisting arrest, theft of a police vehicle——"

"Oh, we'll think of something." She looked appraisingly out at the stream. "You suppose there are any crawfish in that?"

"I don't know." He sighed. "But I wouldn't catch any; the season might be closed."

He lighted cigarettes for them, noting he had only two left, and sat down on the bank. He had to try to think. She lifted her skirt and waded out into the stream, apparently casing it for edible forms of life. She had absolutely perfect legs, he thought.

She turned, saw the appreciative regard, and smiled. "Not bad for three hundred dollars. You can't even tell which one is cork."

"Not from here," he said. "Let's get started. There must be some answer. You didn't kill Torreon, did you?"

"No, of course not." She came over and sat down beside him. "I liked Pepe, he was kind of cute. He was only about five-feet-four in his elevator shoes, but it was all man."

"I've met him," Colby said. "And everybody's heard of him. He was turned on."

"All the way," she agreed, with a fondly reminiscent smile. "Wherever the action was, there was Pepe. And he had this thing about tall blondes. That was the reason I was so startled when I saw my picture in the paper back there—I mean, that they'd found out which one. You could start your own Stockholm with the blondes that have been in Pepe's apartment. So I wasn't particularly worried. . . ."

He could understand that; she fell a little short of being the most outstanding worrier he'd ever run into. And for the whole five days she'd been shut up in that room in the farmhouse and hadn't seen any papers anyway.

"Also," she went on, "nobody would know my real name. He never called me anything but Bougie. He spoke Spanish, of course, and good French, but not much English. He was convinced my name was Candle, so he just translated it because it was easier to pronounce in French. He wasn't touchy or combative about being short, and Torreon means tower in Spanish, so it was kind of a joke—with some overtones of double-entendre —the short tower with the tall candle."

There had been a number of attempts to kill him, because of the revolution and continuing political turmoil in his country and some skepticism over the nine million dollars he appeared to have disbursed for a crate of war-surplus rifles and two dozen hand grenades when he was Minister of Defense, so there was always a bodyguard in the background except in the apartment itself.

That night—or morning, rather—he and Kendall returned to the apartment around four-thirty or five, and the bodyguard left them. It was about an hour later, just at dawn, when they saw they were going to need another bottle of Veuve Cliquot to bridge that parched moment between the evening's last nightcap and the chilled magnum and tin of Beluga caviar awaiting them for breakfast, so they started to the kitchen to get it out of the refrigerator. It was in the other end of the apartment, and they were just going through the salon when the doorbell buzzed.

The door had a small wide-angle lens set in it that afforded a view of the whole hallway outside. Torreon went over to it and looked out, and then asked who it was. He could see, of course, but he always double-checked that way to appraise the speech. Anyone trying to come up to him who spoke French with a Spanish accent was awash in bodyguard before he'd delivered the third syllable.

The voice on the other side of the door said it was a telegram for Monsieur Torreon. It sounded like perfect Parisian French to Kendall, and apparently it did to Torreon also. He took the chain off the door and unlocked it. She could have gone back into the bedroom or the hall, but instead merely stepped over to where she would be out of sight behind the door when it opened.

He opened it about a foot, and there was an odd sort of sound like the *fffssshhh* given off by a punched can of beer, only much louder. Torreon started to collapse. He still had hold of the door, and he swung it back toward Kendall as he fell. She looked down. He had a hand up to his chest, and there was something that resembled a steel spike or bolt sticking out of it right over his heart.

It was so sudden and startling she didn't realize what she was doing; she stepped around the door, right in front of the man.

He had on a postal uniform, cap and everything, and didn't have a weapon of any kind, nothing but that telegram still in his right hand, holding it out—toward her now, instead of Torreon—in a sort of continuing and frozen tableau.

"It was up his sleeve," Colby said. "Homemade gizmo, a high-pressure pneumatic cylinder that fires a steel projectile. There was a man killed with one in Geneva a few years ago."

"That must have been it," she said.

"And you got a look at his face?" he asked, thinking of the weeping gorilla.

"A look at his face? Colby, dear, we weren't two feet apart in a wide-open doorway. Probably that thing up his sleeve would shoot only once, but he was bound to have had a gun with him. But he didn't move; he was kind of glassy-eyed, like a mounted fish, and couldn't seem to get tracked. I didn't have a stitch on, and he just kept saying something that sounded like *jubba-jubba-jubba* and holding out the telegram as if he were looking for someplace to hang it on me or paste it to me."

The poor bastard, Colby thought. With his nerve ends per-manently cauterized, he was probably still going around walking into the sides of buildings and passing cars.

She finally snapped out of the trance herself and slammed the door. She ran to the telephone to call for help, and then realized she didn't have the faintest idea how to get hold of a doctor or hospital at six o'clock in the morning in Paris, and with her limp-ing French she'd never get anywhere. She threw the phone down and ran back to check Pepe, and saw he didn't need help anyway. He was dead. That thing had killed him instantly. She began to cry. So maybe he had stolen everything in his country that wasn't bolted down·or afire, he was a sweet little rooster and she liked him.

Then it began to dawn on her just what kind of spot she was in herself. Even if she could convince the police she didn't have anything to do with the murder, they'd hold her as a material witness—provided the same bunch didn't get her first. Pepe would

94

have regarded risking the latter as a form of idiocy, and the avenging witness bit would only have amused him. So it looked as if a very sound policy here would be that old classic precept for young ladies: get dressed and go home.

But how? They'd be waiting for her. They might get her right out front, or anyway follow her back to the Manning house and do it later. She peered out a window. There was a café across the street with perhaps a dozen men sitting at the tables. The killer wasn't among them, but he wouldn't be, anyway. It would be some of the others; there were bound to be several of them.

So she had to create a diversion, and make sure there were some police in front of the place when she popped out. She got dressed and waited till the streets began to fill up with people going to work. There was a television set in the salon, a big twenty-one-inch model in a hardwood cabinet. She dragged it over in front of a window and peeked down at the sidewalk until there was an open space so she wouldn't kill anybody, and heaved it out.

The apartment was three floors up, so it made an impressive splash. The cabinet disintegrated, and the picture tube exploded, throwing parts all around the street. A pair of passing cars locked fenders, and the drivers began to yell at each other. Whistles blew. Bumpers clanged. Chaos grew, multiplied, and spread outward with that speed and avidity with which only Parisian traffic at a rush hour can scent some minor provocation on which to hurl itself and die gloriously by strangulation. And of course the instant it smashed down there and the flap got under way all the windows in the building flew open and tenants stuck their heads out, to be yelled at by people on the sidewalk for throwing television sets out in the street. *Alors!* You want to kill somebody?

It started raining police. It was at shift-changing time for the traffic officers, and in the jam just below her were two lettuce-baskets bulging with *agents* on their way to their stations. By the time she hit the front door the street was blue with fuzz. She eased out to the perimeter of all the confusion and located a taxi. She had the driver take her clear to Montmartre, then over to the

Left Bank, and finally through the Bois de Bologne, checking to see if she were being followed. She wasn't.

"They located you, though," Colby said. He told her about the man who'd forced his way into the house.

"How did they do it?" she asked. "I'm positive there was nobody behind me. I'd have seen him in the Bois."

"They took the number of the taxi," he said, "and traced down the driver afterward. But where'd the police get that picture, and why did it take 'em so long?"

"I think it's one we had taken in a nightclub. We decided we didn't like it and tore it up, but the photographer probably still had the negative and the police ran it down. And any maître d'hôtel or waiter could have told them he called me Bougie." She dabbled her feet in the water. "Any ideas, Colby?"

"Sure." He wished he had an aspirin. "Disguise you as a four-foot dwarf with rickets. Stay covered. I'm going to try to call Martine from that farmhouse."

"Good. See if you can throw yourself on the commissary."

He eased back to the road, feeling naked and vulnerable in the open. They were bound to have a good description of him on the police networks, and foreigners were rare in rural areas like this. Twice when cars came up behind him he had to fight a jittery impulse to look over his shoulder, but they drove on past.

He walked up the driveway to the house. A small dog ran out from the rear yard and began barking. A middle-aged woman opened the door and regarded him suspiciously, but told the dog to hush.

He smiled and apologized for disturbing her. He was English, he said, working for his company in Paris, and was on his way back from a trip to the Loire valley with his family. They'd had some car trouble down the road——

"A wreck?"

Oh, no, nothing serious; just an engine failure—one of the foskets had lifted in the crenelator. Colby knew little about cars, and cared less, but she wouldn't be any expert either. He could replace it himself, he explained, but he needed the part. If she'd be kind enough to let him use the telephone to call his office——

he'd pay, of course. While he was talking, he took out a fifty-franc note. It wouldn't be over five at the most.

Respect for the franc overcame a centuries-old pessimism toward the motives of all foreigners. She asked him to come in. The telephone was in the hall, near the front door, an old wall-mounted type. She stood nearby while he spoke to the operator, possibly to make sure it was Paris he was calling and not Melbourne or Tokyo.

The phone rang only once on the other end, and was grabbed up immediately. They'd been sweating out the mission, all right. It was Martine.

The woman was still listening. And Flanagan had called him Colby back in the café. "Monsieur Lawrence——" he said.

"Oh, brother! We didn't know whether you'd been killed, or arrested. They didn't get her?"

"No, everybody's fine," he went on in French. "We just had a little car trouble." For the woman's benefit, he explained about the fosket, and asked if somebody would pick one up at the Jaguar agency and have Monsieur Randall bring it out. Could he speak to Monsieur Randall? He needed an excuse to switch to English.

"You're calling from a farm?" she asked.

"Oh, Randall? . . . Yes, I had to. We're both on the lam now." He glanced idly toward the woman. There wasn't a chance she understood English. "I've got her stashed for the moment, but all the fuzz in this end of France is looking for us. She can't move in that Jag, she'd be picked up in a mile. And she can't go back there to the house. Those thugs have got it covered."

"Relax. I've been working on it since the papers came out. Just tell me where you are and leave the rest to me."

He quickly told her how to find the place, and asked, "What about Madame Buffet and the cook? Will they leak?"

"No. I bought 'em off. They liked her, anyway."

"How's Dudley?"

"Better now. The doctor just left."

"He hasn't heard anything yet. Wait'll this morning hits the papers."

"God, that Flanagan. Hang tough, I'm on my way."

Colby thanked the woman, took a couple of ten-franc notes from his wallet, and asked if she could sell him something to eat. His family had been stranded there in the disabled car since late last night, he explained, and everybody was hungry. He accompanied her to the kitchen, and she gave him a loaf of bread, a sausage, and a liter of wine. They didn't have a corkscrew, he said, so she pulled the cork for him, and he insisted they share a glass for her unforgettable kindness and in the interest of continued peace and goodwill between their two great countries. He went back to the road. The door had closed, but he was sure she would be watching from a window. It didn't matter. As soon as he was around the turn the house was out of sight.

An old 2CV came up behind him just as he reached the bridge. He slowed. It went on past and around the next bend a quarter mile ahead, and the road was clear. He plunged off it into the willows. Kendall heard him approach, and turned, her face lighting up with joy at sight of the food. He handed her the bottle. She drank and passed it back to him. They broke the bread and sausage in two and sat down on the bank with the bottle between them.

She took a bite of sausage and waved the chunk of bread toward the encircling willows. "And thou beside me singing in the wilderness—did you get through to the fort?"

"Yes. Martine's on her way."

"Does she have an idea?"

"I think so, but I don't know what. We'll just have to sweat it out till she gets here.'

"Well, with a pair of operators like you two working on it," she said, "I won't worry about it."

"What was the last thing you did worry about? Whether you'd be a forceps delivery?"

98

"Colby, doll, you're on this ledge, on this bank and shoal of time. You reach your hand around a corner, and there's a little bird that puts a new day in it. You use it up, throw the rind back over your shoulder, and stick your hand around again. He puts another day in it, or he craps in it and you're on your way to the showers. Who worries?"

Colby drank some more of the wine and passed her the bottle. "You're from Wyoming?"

"I grew up on a ranch near Jackson Hole, till they had me shod and shipped me east to school."

"Where'd you pick up the judo? And why?" It seemed a little superfluous, like adding bird shot to an atom bomb.

"When I was a kid," she said. "There was what I thought was an advertisement in *The New Yorker*. A big, strapping woman was demonstrating self-defense to a class of girls in a gym, and the caption said, 'With this hold, no man will ever be able to kiss you.' I thought that was wonderful." The bottle gurgled. "By the time I began to doubt the value of it, I was already an expert."

They finished the bread and sausage. She rinsed her fingers in the stream. "A very successful foraging expedition, Trooper Colby. You suppose Martine'll bring additional commissary?"

"She may."

"Good, an army marches on its stomach. Napoleon. Or was it Betty Crocker?" She drained the last of the wine, gave him a dazzling smile, and began to sing, waving the empty bottle.

"We're Sabine Manning's heroes, we are riders of the night,
We are bedroom-oriented, and we'd rather love than fight."

"What's that?" Colby asked. "The Dudley Foundation hymn?"

"Parody of an old army song Sanborn knew. We used to make up new lyrics when we got bored with the job."

"We're her cute surburban houris, our reluctance is so slight
That we're always horizontal, to her publisher's delight.
We're ever combat-ready, not burdened down with clothes,
And mattress-seasoned veterans of a million words of prose."

99

She threw the bottle into the willows, and stretched. "Speaking of the horizontal, I think I'll grab a few winks while there's a lull in the action." She lay back on the bank. Colby gave her his folded jacket for a pillow, and in five minutes she was sleeping peacefully. He looked at her and shook his head. In his life he'd run across a few blithe and unfettered spirits, but Kendall Flanagan was in a class by herself.

He lighted his last cigarette and tried to think, but it only made his headache worse. There was no answer. She couldn't stay here, she had nowhere to go, and she couldn't get there if she did. She had as much chance of going unrecognized anywhere in France as the Eiffel Tower or Charles de Gaulle, and none whatever of leaving it. At any airport or frontier she'd be picked up on sight. And if she were a celebrity now, wait till St.-Médard hit the news; she was going to be the biggest thing since the discovery of grapes. He regarded it with awe. In the long history of French journalism, this was the first story that had everything—a beautiful girl, mystery, international intrigue, wealth, a jet-set playboy, love, clandestine rendezvous, and violent death.

There was nothing to do but wait for Martine. Kendall was sleeping quietly. He eased upstream until he was just below the bridge and found a spot where he could peer out through the last screen of willows and still be invisible from the road. Two or three cars went by, and then a crash-helmeted gendarme on a motorcycle. A few minutes later there was another. He shivered. The whole countryside was probably swarming with them, like vengeful bees. In the next hour there were three more.

The morning was well advanced now and growing quite warm, even here in the shade of the willows. He looked at his watch every few minutes. He heard another car coming downhill around the bend, but it was only an old truck with a high wooden body like a furniture van. Then it was slowing.

He felt a quick stab of fear as it pulled onto the shoulder and stopped near the end of the bridge, directly in front of him. A black-mustached man wearing a beret and a blue denim coverall stepped out of the cab with a bottle of wine and a brown paper bag. They'd stopped for their *casse-croûte*, their coffee break.

Colby heard the other door opening, and at the same moment the man with the bottle gestured downstream and trotted down off the road directly toward his hiding place. He whirled and ran.

Kendall was still asleep in the little glade. He caught her shoulder, and when her eyes flew open he put a hand over her mouth and jerked his head. "Quick!" he whispered. She sprang up. He could already hear footsteps coming down the path toward them. There wasn't time to make it across the glade and run on downstream. He grabbed up his jacket and the briefcase and they sprang into the willows just back of them. As they dropped flat behind the screen of leaves he remembered the motorcycle and swore under his breath, but there was nothing they could do about it now.

He listened, conscious of the pounding of his heart. The man was still coming down the trail beside the stream. Then he froze. Somebody else had come down along the side of the field, the way they had, and was pushing through the willows directly toward them. He was going to pass just beyond their outstretched legs and couldn't fail to see them.

"*L'amour,*" Kendall whispered. "*Vive le sport.*"

He turned swiftly and took her in his arms, his head and shoulders above her to keep her face hidden as he crushed his lips to hers. Her body shifted slightly and the lips parted under his, while her arms locked about his neck and he felt himself drowning in an ocean of blondeness. The footsteps halted just beyond their feet. Blood pounded in his ears as he waited for the stammered Gallic apology and the flight.

Instead, a glacial voice said, "It must be a revival of *Tobacco Road.*"

His head jerked around. Framed in the opening in the willows just beyond the scenic splendor of Kendall Flanagan's left leg was Martine. Beside her was Roberto Giannini. Roberto smiled admiringly. "Always the same old Colby."

"Shut up——!" Colby said. He tried to untangle himself from Kendall's arms and sit up.

"He can't resist the bougainvillea and the wine-dark sea,"

Martine said to Roberto. "Or the music of pigs rooting for truffles."

"Keep your pants on, darling——" Kendall began. At the same moment the dark-mustached man in the beret pushed through the willows from the other direction, halted abruptly, and turned away. "A thousand pardons, Monsieur!" Colby sighed.

Comprehension dawned in Martine's eyes. "Oh—you heard us coming?"

"Of course." He sat up and wearily indicated the man in the beret. "He was the only one I saw getting out of the truck. And we didn't have time to run."

"And you were just doing it for the cause—do I feel like a fink!" Martine smiled sweetly at Kendall, and added, "Such wonderful actors, too. You could have fooled anybody."

"You should catch us when we're eating regularly," Kendall said. She stood up and smoothed down her dress.

Colby had got to his feet. Roberto pushed forward with a broad smile and grabbed his hand. "Good old Colby. And always kissing the most beautiful girls——"

Colby clapped him on the back and cut him off with a hearty greeting of his own. Try to knife me, you gilded beach-boy, and you'll look like a dart board. "It's great to see you! But where's Sabine Manning?"

The mobile Latin face started to freeze, but at the same instant Martine interrupted Colby. "We haven't got much time if we're going to get this thing off the ground." She quickly performed the introductions. The man in the beret was Henri Michel. He owned the truck. Kendall reached for the paper bag and the bottle of wine he was carrying.

"You can eat lunch on the way," Martine said. "Henri will drive."

"Where?" Colby asked.

"Back to the Manning house."

"They'll kill her. They've got it covered."

"No. I've got it all set up——" She started to explain, but Colby caught her arm and led her around the screen of willows out of sight of the others. It had been a long night, and for the moment
102

he'd had it with Dudley's sex novel in all its ramifications. When he tried to take her in his arms, however, he encountered only the thirty-seven elbows and unyielding square corners of a girl who has no intention of being kissed.

"They're different shades," she pointed out. "I'm afraid they might clash."

He scrubbed at his lips with a handkerchief. "I tell you, it was only an act."

"Heavens, dear, I know it was. And real heads-up football, too. But what's that got to do with it?"

He shook his head, wondering bitterly how a man who'd been married twice could still regard logic as a weapon. He must be retarded. There seemed to be only two courses open. He discarded the first, which was to apologize for being right and which in the history of man had never worked yet, and threw everything into the masterful, or bulldozer, approach. In a minute the corners began to melt and flow back into pliable curves and her arms crept up around his neck.

She smiled. "It was quite a night back at the ranch. Especially after we saw the papers."

"There was nothing to be afraid of. I had Flanagan to take care of me."

"That could have been one of the things that made it quite a night back at the ranch."

He was engrossed in the heady business of kissing her again. "Ummmmmhhhhhh?"

"Knowing that she damn well might . . . *Scrape!* The radio's right, you really do need a shave."

"The radio?"

"You're the dangerous-looking thug who speaks French with a Turkish accent and carries a million francs around in a brief-case. But listen—we've only got a minute. We've taken over the project."

"*What?*"

"Merriman's on the verge of collapse, he can't take any more. He was going to run for it, so I made him an offer. For twenty

103

thousand dollars plus expenses we'll finish his book and get Kendall out of France——"

"Good God!" Colby interrupted. "How?"

"Lawrence, please—it's not as hard as it sounds. But there's no time to explain now." She called out to the others. "Everybody, let's go."

They hurried back up the trail, Kendall mincing along as fast as she could on her bare feet and Colby still reeling from Martine's bombshell. They came out to the last screen of willows just below the bridge and peered out. The road was clear.

"Wait till we get set," Martine said. She, Roberto, and Henri ran up onto the road. They opened the rear doors of the van, which had *Michel Frères, Déménagements*, lettered on its side. They looked both ways along the road and beckoned. Colby and Kendall broke from cover and ran. Roberto and Martine had already climbed in, and they helped Kendall up. Colby followed her. Henri grinned at them, said, *"Allons,"* and closed the door. Colby heard him run back and get in the cab. The truck lunged forward and began to gather speed.

There was no light except that seeping in through the cracks around the doors, so it was a minute or two before he could see well enough to make out that the van contained a rather hideous sofa, an old leather-upholstered armchair, a rolled rug, two or three lamps, and a long wooden box that appeared to be empty except for some excelsior in the bottom of it. On one end of the sofa was a bundle of old clothing, apparently workers' blue denims. He saw what she had in mind, and there was a good chance it would work—that far. But the rest of it was staggering.

The truck rattled and swayed, threatening to throw them off their feet. Martine dropped into the armchair. Kendall sat on the sofa, still clutching the bottle of wine and the bag of food, while Roberto seated himself on the floor in front of her.

Colby perched on the corner of the box, dead tired after twenty-four hours of escalating crises, and looked at Martine. "But we'll still have to get her out again."

"No problem," Martine said. "They know she's not in there now—or do if they can read three-inch headlines—so if she never came back, that's the one place in France she couldn't be hiding." She turned to Kendall. "How long would it take you to wrap up the novel? Sanborn's finished, and it's a little over fifty pages."

"Three days, typing it," Kendall replied. "With a recorder and some Dexedrine I could dictate it in twenty-four hours. Or less."

"You're sure?"

"Nothing to it. He's already written the story; I just slather on the mild rich prose. And correct the odd technical bit—he has a tendency to get lingerie mixed up with harness. Why?"

"It's going to take a lot of money to smuggle you out of France. So we finish the book, and Merriman—that is, Sabine Manning—pays for it."

Kendall grinned. "He'll love that."

"He wins, too. If the police get you, he's finished. Apparently they can't trace you to the Manning house, or they would have already. There are some men staked out across the street, but I'm pretty sure they're just the people who're trying to kill you."

"Oh, that's all? Anybody got a corkscrew?"

Roberto produced a Swiss army knife from his pocket. Kendall passed him the bottle. Colby indicated the furniture, and asked Martine, "Where'd you get the props?"

"From Roberto's apartment," she said. As soon as she'd seen the papers and realized they were going to need help—provided Colby and Kendall were able to survive the night without being killed by the kidnapers or arrested—she'd called mutual friends until she located him. He said he could get the moving van; Henri was a friend of his.

When Colby had called, she'd arranged a rendezvous point, and left the Manning house in the Jaguar, followed, of course, by one of the mob that had it staked out. After she'd finally shaken him at a traffic light, she drove through the Bois until she was sure, and met them, leaving the Jaguar parked near the Invalides. She would pick it up again on the way in, so there would be nothing to connect her with the van at all.

So far, so good, Colby thought. "But just how do we slip her out of France? Hide her among a couple dozen other six-foot blondes?"

"Relax." She smiled, with a confident wave of the hand. "We'll come up with it. Heavens, we've got twenty-four hours."

And we've got good old Roberto to help us, Colby thought; that was all the situation had lacked, having your friendly neighborhood pickpocket to hold your coat during the fight. He looked around at Roberto, however, saw the way the latter was eying Kendall, and realized he might have jumped to the wrong conclusion about those two cracks back there beside the stream. Roberto hadn't been trying to knife him with Martine. He'd only been trying to cut his throat with Kendall.

It wasn't that they weren't good friends and boon companions. They were, and had been for a long time. Roberto was amusing company, undeniably talented as a painter—he turned out the best Utrillos since Utrillo—and a prince of a guy who'd give you his last hundred francs. Except that while you were in the bank to see if it was counterfeit he'd disappear with your girl. He respected no right of ownership or prior claim. They were all, in his view, simply part of the public domain, like National Parks, and any old friend zeroing in on a really outstanding girl with Roberto around had only to drop his guard for a few minutes to go home on his shield. But here, apparently, it was Kendall he was after.

He suddenly remembered Miss Manning. Roberto had never answered his question. "Hey, Roberto," he began, and noted, too late, that Martine was violently shaking her head, "where's Sabine Manning?"

The other's head jerked around, the good-looking, normally pleasant face set in a defiant scowl. "How would I know?" he asked. "I'm supposed to be her mother?"

"Okay, okay," Colby said, heeding Martine's signal at last. "I just asked."

"Don't bother. I haven't seen her for six months."

"I came off without a rostrum, but you can use this box if you want to."

"You think I'm going to marry some woman forty-three years old?"

106

Colby was beginning to be a little burned himself. "Why don't we just drop it? Consider I didn't ask."

Roberto muttered something else, while both Martine and Kendall looked at him curiously. Colby shrugged. What was the matter with the sorehead? It wasn't like the old sunny Roberto at all. Of course, it was possible he might have considered Colby was mounting a little guerrilla attack of his own, but he wouldn't have reacted that way. He'd been around too long to needle that easily.

And now that he thought about it, Martine had tried to head him off before, too. She'd abruptly changed the subject. So she had asked the same question and been snapped at herself. Roberto? Acting like a high-school kid or somebody with a guilty conscience? The mystery of Sabine Manning seemed to be growing murkier all the time. She'd been gone only seven months, and if Roberto hadn't seen her for the past six, where was she and what was she doing?

Colby finished shaving with the cordless electric razor Martine had brought in her handbag. It was apparent from their stop-and-go progress and the sounds of traffic around them that they were well into the city now. He and Roberto stripped down to their shirts and shorts, to the accompaniment of Kendall's hushed contralto behind them (". . . she will leave you, and then . . .") and put on the blue denim trousers and jumpers.

Martine studied them appraisingly and buttoned the top button of Colby's jumper to hide his tie. "You'll do," she said.

They put on caps. Kendall corked the bottle of wine and got into the crate; it was long enough for her to lie flat on the bedding of excelsior. Colby dropped his clothing and the briefcase in on her feet and gave her her handbag. Roberto produced a hammer from a toolbox in the forward end of the van, and they began to nail on the short planks forming the top of the crate, leaving enough space between them for good circulation of air. As they put the last one in place, she winked, and closed her eyes. In five minutes, Colby thought, she'd be asleep.

The truck stopped. Henri came back and opened the doors.

Martine got out, followed by Roberto, who would ride in the cab the rest of the way. The doors closed and they rumbled ahead in traffic once more. Colby was aware of increasing tension, and tried to reassure himself. The weeping gorilla was the only one of the mob who'd recognize him, and there was slight chance he'd still be around now that he was known to the people inside the house.

Fifteen or twenty minutes went by. Then he felt the truck swing in to the curb, stop, and reverse a few feet. Cab doors slammed, and there was the sound of footsteps. The rear doors opened. It was Roberto. They were in front of the Manning house, and directly behind them at the curb was Martine's Jaguar.

"We're surrounded," Roberto said softly. "Four men at least. Henri's gone to the door first, so it'll look right."

"How close are they?" Colby asked.

"Two in the next block, pretending to have something wrong with their car. One in a car just ahead of us, and one right across from us, painting. Easel set up on the sidewalk."

"Maybe it's Braque," Colby said bitterly.

"This is the place. Commence," Henri called out from the house. He came down the walk.

"The sofa," Colby said. Taking the box first might attract too much attention. He hopped down, not even glancing across the street, and helped Roberto slide it out. They went up the walk with it, and in the front door.

The salon looked like a back room during the closing hours of a political convention. Dudley, throwing off clouds of cigar smoke, was pacing up and down through a litter of newspapers with a haunted expression on his face, while Martine was snarled in a cocoon of tape as she tried to set up and test a recorder at a table on one side of the room. In front of a phono-radio console tuned to a news broadcast, Madame Buffet and the cook were ecstatically waving their arms and crying out, "Ooooh la la! . . . incroyable . . . formidable . . ." into the torrential delivery of the announcer. As they put the sofa down and started to go back, Dudley blundered into it and sat down. He ground a hand across his face and muttered, "Oh, Jesus Christ!"

"Relax," Colby said. "Everything's under control."

"No savvy, no savvy!" Dudley waved him off and started to pace again. Colby was congratulating himself on his disguise until he realized Dudley had also failed to recognize the English language. "Testing," Martine said, "one, two, three——"

". . . *materializing out of nowhere aboard a truckload of sheep,*" the voice from the radio ran on, charged with lyricism and an awed awareness of history, "*like some ravishing Valkyrie from a Teutonic legend, to descend on this sleepy little village that will never be the same again. . . .*" Colby closed the door and they went back down the walk.

As casually as he could he shot a glance along the street. Roberto had called it with chilling accuracy. On the opposite side in the next block the two men were still standing beside the raised hood of their car, pretending to be interested in its vitals. Just ahead of the truck one man alone in another car didn't appear to be doing anything, but was probably watching them in the mirror. On the opposite sidewalk under the chestnuts, the painter, clad in a smock and beret, appeared to be sketching the house, oblivious to all else. All four would have guns, and they weren't playing—not with this much muscle deployed around the place just on the chance Bougie might try to come back.

Henri was up in the truck, pushing out the crate. Just as they reached it, the painter left his easel and strolled across the street toward them, a tall, cadaverous figure with a hatchet face and the coldest eyes Colby had ever seen. Except once before, he thought, and they belonged to the same man. It was Pascal Decaux.

He tried to still the panic within him; there was little or no chance the man would remember the interview or the drink they'd had together. It was over a year ago, and Decaux had been distraught with grief, anyway, over the matter the police were investigating, the rather grisly suicide of a colleague who had shot himself and then jumped into the Seine with a Peugeot transmission. He couldn't remember all the reporters who interviewed him on these somewhat frequent occasions.

"Anybody got a light?" Decaux asked. Henri snapped his lighter and held it out. Decaux inhaled deeply and swept the interior of the van with an idle glance. "Nice day."

"Very nice," Henri agreed. Roberto and Colby nodded. They gave a tug at the crate, and then wished they hadn't. It was only seven feet long, and maybe he wouldn't notice it.

Decaux looked at it. "Pretty heavy, eh?"

Henri shrugged. "Not too bad. Just books."

"Anybody happen to have the time?"

Colby waited, but apparently he was the only one with a watch. He glanced at it. "Eleven-ten," he said.

"Thanks. . . . Nice watch." Decaux shifted his gaze from the gold-cased Omega Constellation to the threadbare blue denims and then down to the expensive English brogues. Colby wondered if he were dripping blood into them or if it was only sweat. The chill eyes returned to his face. "You're not French?"

"No," Colby said. "Czech."

"I thought so. The accent. But I keep thinking I've seen you somewhere before."

"In Prague, maybe," Colby said. "Czrncrjk's Bar and Grill? Across from the station——"

"Could be. . . . Well, careful of the books." With a wintry

110

smile at his little joke, Decaux nodded to the FRAGILE sign on the side of the crate and went back across the street.

They staggered up the walk with it, every step an agony of suspense. Then they were inside and the door was closed. The confusion seemed to be worse. Either the cook or Madame Buffet had turned up the gain on the news broadcast, apparently on the theory that if it were loud enough Dudley could understand it.

Madame Buffet was attempting to translate. With a heave like Mays cutting off the runner at second, she spread her arms into wings, and cried out, "*Voilà!*—this police—with great astonished he flies into the beaujolais of Monsieur le Maire——!"

"All right, all right!" Dudley clapped his hands to his temples. "Never mind!"

Colby began ripping off the jumper. The cook was near enough his height, only an inch or so under six feet. "Bring in the rest of it," he said to Roberto. "And don't stay together, space it out!"

Martine had already hurried over. "What's wrong?"

"That's Decaux across the street."

"Oh, *no!*"

"And he's spotted me. Or knows he's seen me before. So we can't fast-shuffle him now. He'll count."

"Georges—the cook."

"Right." Roberto and Henri had already gone out, and he'd forgotten to bring in the hammer. He called out to Madame Buffet, "Bring something to open the box with." She hurried toward the kitchen.

Colby cut back the gain on the radio so he could hear himself think. He sat down on the sofa, called Georges over, and began to remove his shoes. He explained what he wanted. "There's not much danger."

"Danger—hah!" Georges snapped his fingers. Gascons were without fear. "But what does it pay?"

"Five hundred francs and a new suit. You'll have to have something to come back in. Make it tonight, take the rest of the day off."

"What'd he say, what'd he say, what is it?" Dudley implored of Martine. Georges and Colby began to undress. Dudley stared

111

at them, his face twitching, and cried out, "For the love of God, will somebody tell me——?"

Martine started to explain. At the same moment Roberto and Henri came in with the overstuffed chair and the rug, while Madame Buffet trotted in from the kitchen with a cleaver. Georges was putting on the blue denims and Colby's brogues. Colby, clad only in shirt and shorts, began prying planks off the top of the case with the cleaver.

"Wrong end," Kendall said from inside, "unless you want me to come out feet first."

"Get to you in a minute," Colby said. "I'm after my pants and some money." He reached in for the briefcase, zipped it open, and took out a sheaf of one-hundred-franc notes. Stripping off ten of them, he handed them to Georges. Dudley's mouth dropped open, and it occurred to Colby this was probably the first he knew that they had recovered the ransom money. "Kendall saved it for you," he said, tossing the briefcase aside. He put the cap on Georges' head and studied the effect. He'd pass, unless Decaux came across the street again.

Roberto and Henri came in with the lamps. Colby slipped up to the front window and parted the drapes an inch to peer out. Decaux was still on the opposite walk, busy at his easel. He shook hands with the two, and said, "Thanks a million. Cover Georges as much as you can till he gets in. Then take it away."

They went out. Colby continued to watch. Decaux appeared to glance at them once as they came down the walk, but remained where he was. Georges got in back. They closed the doors and climbed in the cab. The truck pulled away. Neither of the cars followed it. That could be either good or bad. Maybe they'd suspected nothing at all, but neither would they have any further interest in the truck if they'd guessed what was in the box.

"What do you think?" Martine asked.

"I don't know," he said. "But this is another ball game now, with that guy out there."

"Well, it's only for one day. When the book's finished, we smuggle her out——"

"How?"

"I'm working on it. . . . But let's get her uncrated. She'll want a bath and change before she starts."

Colby whirled and began prying planks off the upper end of the box with the cleaver, forgetting for the moment that he still had no pants on. "What's bugging Roberto?" he asked.

"I don't know," Martine said. "But when I asked him about Miss Manning I thought he was going to bite my head off."

Colby tore off another plank and tossed it aside. One more would do it. "You suppose he stole something from her?"

"I wouldn't think so," Martine said. "She'd give him anything he wanted——"

The doorbell chimed.

Colby started to swing around, his nerves taut, but Kendall was just raising up in the box. He pushed her down and then turned. He was too late. Madame Buffet was already at the door, with Martine right behind her, trying to head her off. She swung it open. Directly in front of them was a man in a postal uniform with a telegram in his right hand, holding it out.

Colby lunged between them. He still had the cleaver in one hand, but he caught the outstretched arm in the other and twisted it down and away from Martine at the same time as he yanked inward. The man shot through the doorway on top of him. He staggered backward and they crashed to the floor beside the box. They hit the briefcase, which fell over, spilling bundles of francs out on the rug. Colby dropped the cleaver and got both hands around the other's forearm, searching for the cylinder and trying to clamp the triggering mechanism. He couldn't feel it. It must be further up. The thing to do was go down the sleeve from inside and get it from the back.

The man, strangely, was offering little resistance, merely making some kind of hiccupping sound. Colby got his hand inside the sleeve of his coat at the shoulder and ran it all the way down until his fingers protruded from the cuff. Nothing.

He withdrew his arm. The man rolled over, removing his face from the pile of banknotes, stared at Colby's untrousered legs and the cleaver lying on the rug just beyond them, and began to slide

113

backward, still making the hiccupping sound. Colby let go and sat up. "Maybe he was just delivering a telegram."

Martine nodded. "I wouldn't rule it out entirely."

The man was still inching backward, white-faced, watching Colby with great staring eyes. He nodded eagerly. "Telegram," he whispered. He set it on the rug between them and backed away from it some more, careful not to make any sudden moves. "Nice telegram . . . all for you. . . ." He felt the box behind him and put a hand up on it to push himself erect. As he did so he was looking down inside it, at Kendall's bare feet stretched out on their bedding of excelsior. With a hoarse cry he whirled and lunged for the door, slamming into Madame Buffet and spilling her on the rug as he went past. He was gone.

Colby slammed the door and locked it, and helped Madame Buffet to her feet. Kendall sat up and began to climb out of the box. Martine turned away from the window, where she'd been watching through the parted drape. "He's on his bicycle and out of sight."

"You suppose he'll tell anybody?" Colby asked, pulling on his trousers and Georges' shoes.

"And be committed for observation? What was the point of trying to get into his coat with him?"

"That was the way they killed Pepe," Kendall explained. "A postman with a gadget up his sleeve."

"Oh."

Kendall turned to Colby. "That man you were talking to out there, that asked for the time——?"

"Pascal Decaux. Hoodlum, professional trigger-man, sort of French version of Murder, Incorporated." He felt the hair begin to lift on his neck. "The voice?"

She nodded. "It could be. Ax-blade for a face, and looks like the terminal stage of something?"

He gestured toward the drapes. "The Sunday painter across the street."

She peered out. So instead of just a consultant called in to remove witnesses, Colby thought weakly, Decaux was the murderer himself. Kendall looked around and nodded. "He's the one."

114

For a moment there was silence. They all looked at each other. Then Martine said, "Well, he still doesn't know you're in here. He's just waiting for you to come back."

Madame Buffet hadn't been able to follow all this English. She appealed to Colby. *"L'homme qui a tué le petit Pepe—le-le swingaire?"* He nodded.

Dudley was leaning numbly against the wall, staring at nothing. His lips moved. "And all I wanted," he whispered, "was to get a book written."

"Cheer up, Merriman." Martine had recovered a little of her old bubbling confidence. "We'll be in production in twenty minutes, and you'll have your book by tomorrow morning. . . ." She caught sight of the telegram then, still lying on the rug, and stooped to pick it up. "After what the poor man went through to deliver it, we could at least look at it. It's for you. From Nice."

Dudley shook his head. "I don't know anybody in Nice."

She tore it open and unfolded it. It seemed to be several pages. She turned back to the last one. "Hey! It's from Miss Manning."

Oh-oh, Colby thought. There was utter silence for a moment as she flipped the sheets back and began to scan the first. "Merriman," she said gently, "you'd better sit down."

"Go ahead," Dudley said. "Nothing else can happen to me."

"Monsieur Merriman Dudley, Seven *Rue* et cetera, et cetera, et cetera," she said. "The text reads: *Urgent you retain services best available public relations firm to commence immediate task of complete eradication my unfortunate image as writer of sexy drivel, and simultaneous promotion of emergence new Sabine Manning, historian, submarine archaeologist, and student of ancient Mediterranean cultures Stop After six months intensive work, research now essentially complete for my new book, an exploration in depth of mysterious and hitherto unexplained similarities between bronze metalwork of Phoenician galleys circa one hundred and fifty B.C. and those of latter-period Roman republic, hinting strongly at cartels or industrial espionage transcending national loyalties before and during Third Punic War Stop—*"

Dudley collapsed on the sofa with his face in his hands. Martine looked at him with concern, but went on: "——*Stop You can readily understand that in view of great importance of this work it is imperative that its appearance be unstigmatized by even any residual impression in public mind linking name Sabine Manning with previously published sex rubbish*——"

She broke off. Dudley had been quietly sobbing, but now he began to giggle. "Punic Wars," he tittered. "Writing a book about the Punic Wars." With a great howl of laughter, he dropped to his knees on the rug in front of the couch.

"Get some water," Colby snapped to Madame Buffet and lunged for him. Hauling him up, he dropped him back on the sofa and slapped him across both sides of the face. "Snap out of it!" The laughter cut off, and Dudley stared at him without comprehension. "Haul ass," he muttered. "Call Air France——" His eyes closed and he slumped back.

"Poor Merriman," Martine said.

"And he almost had it made." Kendall spread her hands. "Where do we go from here?"

"Maybe I'm a masochist," Colby said, "but is there any more?"

"Yes," Martine said. She continued reading. "*Cannot emphasize too strongly that all publicity releases must, repeat must, deplore present shoddy state of writing and publishing worlds in their pandering to and promotion of unhealthy preoccupation with sex Stop Yacht now undergoing repairs and refitting here, so will be personally available coming week or ten days for cocktail parties, interviews and/or press conferences as arranged by chosen public relations firm Stop*——"

There was a sudden outcry somewhere in the rear of the house, followed by a crash and a volley of indignant French. Colby whirled. Madame Buffet had gone to the kitchen after water, but the footsteps pounding up the hallway toward them were too heavy to be hers. "Down, get out of sight!" he snapped to Martine and Kendall as he jumped back against the wall beside the door. They dropped behind the sofa and box. The man shot into the room, drawn automatic thrust out before him, saw nobody but the unconscious Dudley, and started to turn. Colby pushed off

116

the wall and hit him from behind with the hardest diving tackle he had ever made.

The man's head snapped back with a whiplash motion and then banged against the floor as they came down. The gun came to rest on the rug in front of them. Colby grabbed it up by the butt, rapped him on the head with it and then once more for insurance, and sprang up. Kendall and Martine emerged from their hiding places. "If he comes to," he said to Kendall, "bounce him off the wall."

Gun in hand, he ran down the hallway. In the kitchen, Madame Buffet was just getting off the floor, making too much forceful and bitter comment to be seriously hurt. He shot past her, locked the door leading into the alley, and threw the bolt. Turning, he helped her up. "You all right?"

". . . littérature . . . merde . . . !"

"Is there another outside door?"

She shook her head. ". . . maison de fous. . . ."

Colby yanked open drawers and closets, grabbed up an extension cord and a handful of dish towels, and ran back to the salon. The man was still out, with Kendall standing over him. He tied his legs together with the electrical cord and used the dish towels to bind his hands and gag him. Dudley stirred and sat up.

Colby reached for a pack of cigarettes on the table beside the recorder and lighted one, conscious of exhaustion and utter defeat. For twenty-four hours they had been plugging successive and ever-bigger holes in a dike that had been doomed to begin with, and now they were finished. Decaux knew Kendall was in here, and there was no way to get her out. The novel was worthless. So was their agreement with Dudley, and the six-thousand-dollar check they already had.

Martine still had the telegram. As calmly as though there had been no interruption, she flipped over to the last page and read it: "*Already have photographic coverage of expedition yacht and personnel adequate for all publicity purposes Signed Sabine Manning.*"

For a moment no one moved. Then Dudley dropped to the

floor and began stuffing the money back in the briefcase. He zipped it and headed for the stairs.

"Where are you going?" Martine demanded.

"Brazil," he said. "For a start."

"Merriman!" Her eyes flashed. "Come back here."

"You may be crazy——"

"You'd go off and leave Kendall here to be killed?"

"What can I do about it?"

"Carry out the terms of your agreement. We need help to get her out of France, and it takes money."

He stared at her. "You expect me to pay out more money for that goddam manuscript—*now*? After that telegram?"

"Merriman Dudley, we've been friends a long time, but if you go out that door we're finished. We got that reporter out of your hair, then Lawrence got Kendall back, and the two of them saved your thirty thousand francs. So now it's all for nothing because you want to chicken out and run. After all, what have we done for you lately?"

"*Sauve qui peut*," Colby said bitterly.

"What does that mean?"

"Take up the ladder, mate, I'm aboard."

"Look——" Dudley protested.

"Never mind," Martine said to Colby, "let him go." She reached for her purse. Taking out her checkbook, she addressed Dudley with icy disdain, "But before you do, I want to buy that manuscript."

"*What?*"

"Get your records and tell me exactly what you paid Sanborn and Kendall for writing it. I'll give you a check payable to Sabine Manning for the full amount, and it's mine."

"Why?"

"Never mind why. Either honor your agreement or sell me the manuscript and get out of my way."

Colby watched with awe. She was fantastic—not only as an actress, but as a gambler. This was the coldest bluff he had ever seen.

"Listen!" Dudley shouted. "You read the telegram! She's not

118

nly gone nuts, but she's in Nice! She could walk in here any minute!"

"We could still have it finished before she gets here."

"What the hell good is it? We've run out of time. There's no vay we can keep her from finding out about it——"

Martine interrupted. "Then you *will* sell it?"

"Martine—if we delivered it to Holton Press in the next five ninutes." Dudley took a deep breath and tried again, desperation written on his face. "Look—they've got a sex novel we say she ust finished, and in every newspaper in the Western hemisphere he's on her soapbox trying to have it outlawed. They just might wonder——"

"Could you just give me a simple yes or no?"

"How do you expect to sell it?" Dudley cried out. "Without Sabine Manning's name on it you won't get your money back."

"I'm waiting, Merriman."

Up against the unanswerable, Dudley broke at last. "All right." He slumped down on the sofa. "I'll stay."

"That's better." She smiled. "I appreciate your vote of confidence."

"But let's be sure we understand the agreement. I pay for the muggling operation now, but the twenty thousand is no-cure-o-pay. You don't get a dollar of it unless that manuscript goes o Holton Press with Miss Manning's name on it."

"Fair enough. We wouldn't have taken the job unless we hought we could do it." Her voice was confident, but the face houghtful as she glanced at the man on the floor, and then oward Colby. Their eyes met, the knowledge unspoken between hem. Now that Decaux knew Kendall was in here, getting her out alive was going to take something approximating a miracle.

And there was the further matter of keeping him and his mob from getting in. They had a gun—two of them, in fact—and both utside doors were locked. But there still remained the windows.

As though she'd been following his line of thought word for word, Martine asked Dudley, "Do all the windows have shutters?"

"Yes," he said. "But anybody could tear one off."

"Not without noise. Close and fasten all of them except that

119

one." She nodded to the one looking on the street. "They won't try to break in there with a street light in front of the house, and we want to be able to see out."

"Okay." Dudley went out.

She turned to Kendall. "Now, where would you like to work?"

"My same room. Second floor, just down the hall from the office."

"Good. The recorder's ready to go. Will you need any help running it?"

"I hope not. I'm going to dictate the first four hours from a hot bath."

Martine opened her purse again. "Here's a Dexedrine so you won't fall asleep." Kendall took the tablet, picked up the recorder, and hurried up the stairs.

Colby reached for another cigarette. "Remind me never to play poker with you."

Martine's face was still overlaid with that slightly frowning, thoughtful expression. "It wasn't entirely bluff. I would have bought it."

Colby stared, with a feeling he was lost. He and this girl had an ability to communicate without speech, up to a point, but now she was ahead of him. They'd had to hold Dudley to his agreement because they couldn't abandon Kendall. In addition to the fact they both liked her, they were the ones who'd brought her into this death trap. But the manuscript?

"If you want to start a fire," he said, "lighter fluid is cheaper."

"No," she said musingly. "You're falling into Merriman's trap, the canalized line of reasoning. The key to the whole thing, of course, is still Miss Manning, but no longer in the same way. The question is who is she now? What is she?"

"Instant Suetonius. We know that. Schliemann with fins."

"No. I mean, precisely what happened to her?"

"The crusade against sex? It's obvious, isn't it?"

"Not to me," she said.

"Look . . . she's a plain, very shy woman, the eternal wall-flower, rejected by everybody. She gets hurt, sure, but never really clobbered because she stays in her shell where they can't reach her. Then Roberto rolls her in the hay, she loves it, falls for him like a ton of bricks, begins to open up and come out, as vulnerable as a shucked oyster, and bang—she gets it right between the eyes. That bastard, as many women as he's left, you'd think he could do it with a little grace."

"I'm not sure you're right." She smiled. "But I'm interested to hear you're an authority on how to leave women."

"I'm just a good listener. I was in Korea with a guy who was going to write a book on it."

"Did he?"

"I don't know, he could never seem to sharpen his timing. The last I heard, he'd left four, and his alimony bill was six thousand dollars a month. But why don't you agree with it?"

"I'm not sure. Just a hunch. It's too pat, anyway, a cliché."

"Sure. But what's a cliché except something that happens all the time? It's standard situation nine-D right out of the stock bin, but it's still true. She was probably pleading with him when he walked out on her and he got bugged and said something cruel, and the human race goes down swinging. She was right back where she started, only now it was a thousand times worse because she'd begun to think that somebody could care for her——"

"When do we get to the snowstorm, when her father won't let her in the house with the baby?"

"Well, what do you think happened?"

"I don't know," she said, still lost in thought. "But Roberto doesn't quite ring true, and neither does her telegram." She stood up. "Give me about half an hour. I'll be up in the office."

Colby checked the man on the floor. He was heavy-shouldered, dark, about thirty, still unconscious but breathing all right. Colby pulled him over against the wall out of the way, looked at him again, shrugged, and put a sofa pillow under his head. He was just an instrument, one of the workmen.

Decaux was still across the street, along with one of the cars, deadly, inevitable, as impervious to annulment or modification as planetary motion. Colby let the drape fall back in place. Answer? Where was it? Smuggling Kendall out of France had sounded like an impossible project, but that was the good old days. Try smuggling her into the next block. Dudley came back. Colby gave him the automatic.

"Yell, if you hear anything," he said. He went in search of Madame Buffet, retrieved his bag, and had a shower and a change of clothing. When he got to the office Martine had the Michelin road map of France spread out on the desk, along with her address book and a scratchpad covered with figures and what looked like several names with telephone numbers. She was just putting down the phone.

He perched on a corner of the desk and reached for a cigarette. "Ogden Nash was right. You can't get there from here."

"Sure you can." She leaned back in the chair, tapping her teeth with the end of a pencil. "But to dispose of the easy part first, let's start a half-mile from here. North Africa's the best bet. It's far enough away, and she can catch a plane or ship to the States with no trouble. *D'accord?*"

"Sure. But how does she get there?"

"The same way you get in the Social Register or a floating crap game—money and connections." She shuffled through her notes. "Here's a number to call in Nice, a man named Jules Clavel. He has a finger in all kinds of rackets there and in Marseille. He

122

made a fortune smuggling out of Tangier just after the war, and still has some good fast boats and contacts all along the African coast. His mistress is a friend of mine, and she's already called him to establish our credentials. But before we phone, maybe you'd better knock on Kendall's door and see if she can give us an approximate time she'll be through."

"Which is hers?"

"The next one on the right."

The door was closed, but he could hear the murmur of her voice inside. He knocked twice before she heard him. "Come in," she called. He pushed open the door. The black dress and her slip were on the bed, and an open suitcase on a stand at the foot of it. There was a typewriter on a stand near the dresser. The drapes were tightly drawn across the window, but the bathroom door was ajar. Through it he could hear the splash of water and her voice.

". . . *the immemorial dark tide of ecstasy and desire and the wild sweet singing in the blood period paragraph*—who is it?"

"Colby. Can you give us a rough idea when you'll be finished? We've got to set up a timetable."

"Hmmmmm—let's see—forty-six pages to go. Seven tomorrow morning at the latest. *Quote Oh, Greg, Greg, Greg, unquote she whispered comma delirious with rapture comma—*"

"Thanks," he said. He started out.

"*—melting under the touch of hands that left their tracery of fire*—oh, Colby."

He turned. "What?"

"In my bag there's another bottle of bath salts, Prince Matcha-belli, I think it is. Will you hand it to me? *Quote Oh, God, darling, unquote she gasped, quote I love it, I love it—*"

He rooted through a welter of nylon and lace and located it while she went on dictating. "Here you go." He reached it in around the door.

"*—darling, darling, darling*—you'll have to come a little closer."

"You mean me," he asked, "or Greg?"

"You . . . down a little . . . not quite yet . . . oh, go ahead and dump it in, I'm submerged."

He went in. She was up to her shoulders in foam, the microphone held in one hand. The recorder was on a chair beside the tub, the clipboard with the rest of Sanborn's manuscript propped up against it. She tore off a page and let it fall among the half dozen already scattered around the floor.

"——*comma unquote the words squeezed and ragged with passion comma torn from her*—about a third of it, Colby——"

He uncapped the bottle and shook it over the tub. "You want me to stir it?"

"No, that's all right." A satiny and foam-bejeweled leg emerged, swishing the surface. "——*by his inexorably mounting cadence and that final swamping of all her senses under the onrushing flood of desire that was like torment demanding release*—could I have a puff on that?"

"Sure." He perched on the side of the tub and held the cigarette between her lips. "Does writing that stuff have any anaphrodisiac effect? I'd be off sex forever."

"No." She smiled and exhaled smoke. "After awhile you don't even hear it." She took another puff, pressed the microphone button, and went on, "——*comma aflame with that age-old exultation in the terrible urgency of his need for her*—thanks, Colby."

"Not at all." He set the bottle on the chair and got up.

"——*Period With a gibbering little cry of unbearable ecstasy comma she thrust her hips upward against him comma*——"

He went back to the office. He dialed the number in Nice, and in a few minutes was through to Clavel. He introduced himself and said he was a friend of Martine Randall.

"I know," Clavel broke in. "What do you need?"

Transportation, Colby replied. For himself? No, for a young lady whose doctor had prescribed a change of scene; she'd developed a strange allergy to crowds and to people wearing blue, and he thought perhaps North Africa——

"I've got a hunch I know who you mean," Clavel said. "We have newspapers here too. Any particular place?"

"Anywhere she could catch a ship or plane to the United States without a stop in France. She'd need an entry stamp—and visa if it's called for—to clear her on the way out."

"We've got one of the top men. Passport, UN credentials—you name it."

"She can use her own passport once she's out of France."

"We've got a boat leaving for Rabat Saturday night. How about that?"

This was Thursday; Saturday would be perfect, with plenty of leeway for getting there. "Good. Where could you pick her up?"

"There's a cove west of Cannes. You'd better write this down." He gave directions and exact mileage. Colby jotted it down. "Have her there at nine p.m."

"Check," Colby said. "And what's the tab?"

"Twenty-five thousand francs."

"Okay. Now, there's one more thing; there may be a price being offered around to take her somewhere else——"

"If we're talking about the same girl, there is."

"If the twenty-five thousand doesn't top it, say so now. I want to pay her fare all the way across."

"Forget it. I know the guy that's after her, and we don't do business with him. Have her there, the captain'll wait five minutes, and that's it."

"He won't have to wait at all. If she's not there it'll be in the papers."

He hung up and repeated the conversation to Martine. "Good so far. Now, from here to Cannes?"

"That's the easiest part of it." She went on to explain. Roberto would take her; she'd already talked to him. He was out now looking for the vehicle, one of those pickup trucks with the camper body on it. She thought he could get a good used one for around six thousand francs.

Colby nodded. "Still good."

"So. . . ." She smiled. "We've solved everything but the problem. Any ideas?"

"No. You couldn't smuggle a hamster out of here as long as he's there, and you can't move him."

"We have to move him, that's the only solution. So approach it from there. What would induce him to go away?"

"Nothing on earth. Till he gets her. God knows how many people he's killed, but this is the first time there's ever been a witness——"

"Wait a minute!" she interrupted. She leaned back in the chair. Seconds stretched out as she continued to stare straight ahead of her, biting her lip. Then she sat up abruptly. "Colby! We've got it!"

She explained. It took five minutes, while he listened with increasing awe.

He whistled. "Mother, dear. But can we cast a production like that?"

"Why not? All we need is Henri, Roberto, the moving van, and four plain-clothes cops. I can do it on the phone in twenty minutes."

Colby made a complete tour of the house from the attic downward to be sure there was no place they could get in after it was dark. When he came to the salon, he peered out. Decaux was still there, as well as one of the cars.

Dudley indicated the bound man lying against the wall. "I think he wants to say something. Keeps trying to make a noise."

Colby removed the gag and was greeted by a geyser of abuse in a Marseille accent.

"What'd he say?" Dudley asked.

"The only thing printable is that he wants to go to the john."

"The hell with him."

"Oh, I'll take him. Give me the gun and you untie him. Just his arms, he can hop."

Dudley loosed the bonds and stepped back. "Nearest one's Miss Manning's bathroom. Through that door and down the hall."

Colby followed the man's kangaroo progress with the gun centered on his back. Miss Manning's rooms consisted of a book-lined study, a large bedroom carpeted with a shaggy white rug, and a bathroom that had been modernized and done over in coral and black. He looked around the study and bedroom, thinking of

126

the unhappy spinster now completely withdrawn and made bitter by the final rejection. It was a shame.

They came back. "You are kidnapers," the man said angrily as Dudley tied his hands again.

"That we are," Colby agreed. "But who knows, perhaps you will return to your friends tomorrow."

"You are dirty——" A mouthful of dish towel cut off the rest of his comment.

Madame Buffet made sandwiches and opened some bottles of wine. Kendall took hers in her room while she went on dictating. Colby and Martine ate at the desk in the office. She gave him a report. Everything was falling into place for H-hour, eight tomorrow morning.

She'd located four friends, three of them bit players in films, who were willing to impersonate inspectors from the Quai des Orfèvres for a half-hour for five hundred francs. Two of them looked a little like Jean Gabin, and it was one of these, Émile Voivin, who would have the speaking part. She'd rehearsed him in it. Roberto had called. He'd found a used pickup camper that could be had for fifty-two hundred francs. A cruise ship named the *Heraldic* was calling at Rabat a week from Saturday, bound for New York by way of Gibraltar, the West Indies, and Nassau. She'd made a reservation for first-class passage in Kendall's name.

Roberto arrived in a taxi shortly after four P.M. They gave him the money for the truck, for the provisions he would need, and for Kendall's steamship ticket, which he would pick up after he was certain he wasn't being followed.

"They won't follow anybody now," Colby said. "They know where she is."

They brought out the map of Paris and briefed him. "You'll rendezvous at this point on the Rue Céleste at eight a.m.," Martine went on. "That's only four blocks from here and you don't have to go through any traffic lights or cross any arterials to get here, which could wreck the timing. You park the pickup truck and get in the van with Henri. Voivin and the other three men will be in another car.

"Lawrence will arrive at the same time in my car. He'll get in the back of the van. Henri will have an extra-large coverall he can put on over his suit, and a beret, the same things you'll be wearing. As soon as he's gone over it once more with Voivin, Henri will drive the van around here, going very fast once you've turned into this street and you're visible to Decaux and his men. Voivin will leave exactly two minutes later. The timing has to be very precise. If Voivin gets here too soon we won't fool him, and if he's too late it could be very dangerous. Everything clear?"

"Yes," Roberto said.

"Good. Here are the instructions for finding the cove after you get to Cannes. You can keep the truck, or sell it, whichever you wish. See you in the morning."

Roberto left. Martine had found another recorder, one with a foot switch, and she began to transcribe the first of Kendall's tapes. It seemed a waste of effort to Colby, typing a worthless manuscript, but they couldn't sit and do nothing. The suspense of waiting for eight A.M. would have them going up the wall.

Decaux disappeared from in front of the house, but there were two cars on station and the state of siege went on as night began. Madame Buffet made coffee. Dudley continued to watch in the now-darkened salon, alert for the first warning sounds of attempted entry. The house was silent except for the clatter of Martine's typewriter in the office. Colby took over. He was dead tired, now close to forty hours without sleep. He took one of Martine's Dexedrine tablets and came to life again.

Shortly after eleven the cook arrived in a taxi, identified himself, and was let in, carrying an armful of newspapers. *Voilà!*

WHO IS BOUGIE? the headlines cried. WHERE IS BOUGIE? DID BOUGIE KILL PEPE? Was Bougie protecting her lover, the real assassin? Was Bougie a Russian spy, a Magyar princess, a reincarnated Viking, a publicity stunt by some American cereal manufacturer? At various times and places Bougie had spoken French with an American accent, English accent, German accent, Balkan accent, Vaudois accent, and the accents of four different provinces of France. The photograph was emblazoned on the front pages of most of them, and two carried a picture of Colby drawn by a police artist from the descriptions of eyewitnesses in the café at St.-Médard. He looked like the man who is always questioned by police after a series of mysterious stranglings. There was a picture of the café, with a dotted line showing the trajectory of the gendarme, and several photographs of Pepe Torreon, one without a blonde.

The briefcase now contained two million francs and bore an indecipherable coat of arms. Little credence was given in most circles, however, to the theory that Colby might have been implicated in the assassination of Rasputin.

An arrest was expected momentarily.

The night wore on. The cook relieved Dudley, patrolling the downstairs areas. Martine typed. Colby took over again, mechanically pounding out words that had lost all meaning. Martine was dozing in a chair and he had just rolled page three hundred and eighty-one into the machine when Kendall came down the hall, dressed in blue pajamas and carrying the other recorder. She set it on the desk in front of him and reached for a cigarette.

"The baby's born," she said. It was six forty-five A.M.

Martine was instantly alert. She went to the head of the stairs and called out to Dudley, who came running up, followed almost immediately by Madame Buffet and Georges with a bottle of champagne and six glasses.

Martine indicated the pile of manuscript. "Three hundred and eighty pages typed, and one more roll of tape on Kendall's machine. We'll have it ready by noon."

Dudley looked dazed. He gave a wondering shake of the head. "Oh, boy," he whispered, "if she'll only stay away a little longer."

Kendall raised her glass. "To biogenesis."

They drank several toasts. Dudley and Georges went back downstairs. Colby and Martine explained the proposed escape route to Kendall, and gave her the folder containing her passport and the twenty-five thousand francs for Clavel's boat captain.

"Get your bag packed," Martine said, "but stay in those pajamas—it'll be easier to put on the coverall. There's nothing to it

129

the rest of the way, if we can just get you out of here. It all depends on whether we can move Decaux. Be downstairs and ready to go by ten till eight."

Kendall left. Colby thought of something else. "You wouldn't have any sleeping pills in that pharmacy of yours, would you?" he asked Martine.

"Sure. Why?"

"Give me three of 'em. For our friend downstairs."

They went down to the salon. Colby sent Madame Buffet to the kitchen for a glass of water, a hammer, and a screwdriver. He asked Dudley to hold the gun on the man while he unbound his hands and then re-lashed them against his body so he could lie on his back.

"Okay, in with him," Colby said. They lifted him into Kendall's crate. Colby removed the gag.

"What's that for?" Dudley asked.

Colby indicated the pills in Martine's hand. "There's no way to tie him in there so he can't kick around and make a lot of noise. So we just put him to sleep."

"It'll be interesting to see how you get him to swallow them," Martine said.

"He'll swallow or drown," Colby replied in French.

"But how are you going to get 'em in his mouth?" she asked. The man's string of curses had cut off and he'd clenched his jaw as soon as he saw the pills.

"Easy," Colby said. He knelt beside the box and took the hammer and screwdriver from Madame Buffet. He inserted the screwdriver blade between the man's lips, selected an incisor, and drew back the hammer. "Just knock out a tooth," he went on in French, "and drop 'em in. If he swallows the tooth too it won't hurt him." The man's mouth opened in a great hippo yawn, the pills fell in, and were washed down with a swallow of water.

Colby retied the gag, and began to nail the lid on.

It was seven thirty-five. "Time to go," he said.

He took a last look through the window drapes. Decaux was nowhere in sight yet, but a car with one man in it was parked across the street. Martine gave Colby the car keys, and silently held up crossed fingers. He went out and got in the Jaguar.

A block away he met Decaux coming along the opposite sidewalk with his easel and box of paints. He sighed with relief. Decaux was infinitely the most dangerous of them, but he was probably the only one with the intelligence and daring to see the opportunity and seize it. He went on two more blocks and turned toward the Bois de Bologne. There was probably less than one chance in a hundred he was being followed, but he had to eliminate that one.

It was a beautiful morning, crisp and clear with pockets of opalescent mist that reminded him of Turner and flashes of crimson and gold on every side. His own personal choice for Heaven, he thought, would be an eternity of successive hand-picked October days in Paris. After, of course, the last automobile in it had been hunted down and beaten to death with flails. He doubled back and forth across the Bois at different speeds for ten minutes, and stopped to smoke a cigarette. Nobody was following him. He drove back to the Rue Céleste. The van was already parked at the rendezvous point, and Roberto was just pulling in with the pickup. It was five of eight.

They greeted him warmly and with suppressed but still evident excitement. "Take a look," Roberto said proudly, opening the rear door of the camper body.

It held two bunks with mattresses and pillows, and a shelf at the forward end supported a radio and reading lamp. There were small windows on each side, well-covered with dark green curtains. Most of the floor space between the bunks was taken up with boxes of food and a small icebox. Once she was in there she was out of sight all the way to the boat.

"Good," Colby said.

Henri sighed. "Lucky Roberto."

"Well, I offered to cut cards, didn't I?" Roberto said. "If it was all right with your wife——"

"The gambler!"

Roberto locked the door. They went back to the van. Colby opened the doors, hopped up inside, and began to pull on the big blue denim coverall. He put on the beret. A Peugeot pulled in to the curb behind them and four men got out. Colby knelt on the tailgate and asked, "Which one is Monsieur Voivin?"

"Me," said the one who'd been driving. He was a heavy-set man in early middle age with wiry gray hair and a totally masculine but still somehow gentle face. He looked like a cop, all right, and a good one, Colby thought. He introduced himself and brought out an envelope containing two thousand francs. He passed it out to them, and spoke to Voivin.

"Let's run through it once, the way Martine explained it on the phone. You pull up right behind us. Take it from there."

Voivin ran through his part without hesitation. "Perfect," Colby said. "In two minutes exactly." They got back in the Peugeot.

He spoke to Henri. "And the gasoline?"

"Less than a liter. Four kilometers at the most."

"Good. And it's already been reported stolen?"

"An hour ago. Driven off from an address on the Boulevard Montparnasse." He grinned. "The ignition switch is jumpered."

Colby nodded. "Leave the engine running, the wires twisted together but out of sight under the dash."

"D'accord."

Colby looked at his watch. It was three minutes after eight. He felt the stirring of butterfly wings. "Take it away."

The doors closed. They began to move.

They turned right. They were on the Avenue Victor Hugo. He looked around the dim interior of the van. It contained a dis-assembled bedstead, a chest of drawers, an old trunk, and a couple of small rugs. Traffic snarled around them. They swung right again, into the Rue des Feuilles Mortes, and began to gather speed. Decaux would have seen them by now and recognized the van. Brakes squealed and they swerved in to the curb.

Cab doors banged and there was the sound of running foot-steps. The rear doors opened. Colby jumped down, not even looking toward Decaux, and the three of them strode up the walk. The front door opened as they hit the steps, and closed be-hind them. Everybody was in the salon. Martine was peering through a tiny opening in the drapes. They grabbed up the crate.

Madame Buffet swung the door open again. They squeezed through and she closed it.

They hurried down the walk, trying to keep stride. Decaux merely glanced toward them once, held up his thumb for perspective, and went on sketching. Wondering what kind of collection of damned fools he's dealing with, Colby thought, believing they could draw him away with as obvious a decoy as this. Bougie wouldn't be in the box. But still—why the hurry?

They set it on the tailgate and shoved. It slid on. This was where it had to be when the carload of detectives swung into the street, merely sitting there, with only Decaux knowing it had come from the house. Henri hopped up inside to help slide it back. He was out of sight of Decaux now, and facing back toward the avenue. He nodded. Voivin was coming.

he Peugeot swerved into the curb and stopped some six feet behind them. Colby and Roberto, still shoving on the box, turned at the sound. They exchanged a quick glance and assumed attitudes of studied nonchalance. The four men piled out of the car and onto the sidewalk.

Voivin gestured crisply toward the house. "Paul-Jacques, cover the back." One man trotted back along the side of the house toward the rear door. "Let's go," Voivin said to the others. "Maurice will remain inside the front door and Auguste and I will start with the attic."

They had taken two or three strides up the walk when Voivin stopped with a sort of frowning double take and looked back at the van. He waved the others on and came back. Stepping off the curb just behind Colby and Roberto, he glanced inside. "What are you men doing here?" he asked.

Roberto swallowed but managed an uncertain smile. "Well——"

"Uh—just moving stuff," Colby said. "We're in the moving business—like it says—the sign——" He couldn't seem to get himself turned off.

The gray eyes probed. "Foreigner, aren't you?"

Colby nodded. "Czech."

"Let's see your identity card."

"Well, wait a minute," Colby said. "Who are you?"

"*Police Judiciaire.*" Voivin reached in his coat pocket and flashed identification in the palm of his hand. It was only an art study of a markedly uninhibited young lady, but Colby looked properly impressed. He produced his driver's license. Voivin glanced at it and handed it back.

"What's in that box?" he asked.

"Books," Colby said.

"Dishes," Roberto replied at the same instant.

134

"Just stuff——" Henri began, but stopped. Almost in time.

"Oh?" Voivin stepped closer, and studied the box with a speculative eye, obviously gauging its length. "And you just brought it out of that house?"

"Oh—no," Colby said. "It didn't come out of this house. We picked it up over in—in——"

"Well, what are you doing here?"

"We're—uh—that is, we're delivering it here."

"Oh." Voivin gave him a suspicious glance, but shrugged. "I thought you were putting it on the truck."

"Oh, no," Colby said. "Taking it off."

"Okay." Voivin turned away indifferently and started up the walk again. He turned. "Well? What are you waiting for? Take it in. It's all right."

"Sure. Thanks," Colby said. "We've got some other stuff—we'll take in first——"

"Why don't you turn off your engine?"

"It's hard to start," Roberto said. "Weak battery——"

Voivin was still staring at them suspiciously. Henri began shoving the other things toward the rear. Roberto and Colby grabbed up random pieces of the bedstead and started up the walk, followed by Henri. Voivin turned again and went on toward the front door. When he disappeared inside they all turned and looked longingly back at the truck, but Colby jerked his head and they went on. *Not yet; wait'll he gets upstairs.*

Decaux should have it now. They'd had to get her out because the police had finally learned who Bougie was and were coming to search the place. Bougie *was* in the box, and in about five minutes or less Inspector Voivin of the *Police Judiciaire* was going to figure it out for himself.

He and Roberto went through the door. Voivin and the two men were standing to one side out of the way. Colby ran to the drape to peer out. Decaux was still calmly painting. And he'd heard every word; he'd simply seen through it, and it wasn't going to work. But Henri was still on the walk. He came in. The door closed. Colby's hands clenched. *Come on—come on——!*

Decaux waved an arm and ran for the door of the cab. The

135

man who was in the parked car leaped out of it, slammed the rear doors of the van, and ran around to the other side, making it onto the running board with a flying leap as Decaux gunned it ahead. Colby felt all the breath ooze out of him at once and he wanted to slump down. As the truck roared ahead into the next block another car fell in behind it. Colby turned and nodded.

All the tension in the room snapped at once and there was pandemonium. Martine fell in his arms. "Darling! We did it, we did it!" She pulled his head down and kissed him.

Voivin had headed for the door. With his hand on the knob, he turned to Colby, "Now?"

"Yes," Colby said. "Don't try to stay close. Just watch for a traffic jam."

He and the other men ran out. Roberto was throwing off his denim coverall. He kicked it aside and shot for the door. "Go down the Rue Mon Coeur," Martine said. "It's nearer."

"Back in three minutes." He ran out. Colby was unbuttoning his own coverall. He stepped out of it and handed it to Kendall. While she was pulling it on, Martine worked the beret over her pinned-up hair, poking loose strands up inside. Colby drew the drapes and looked out. Except for the one the man had abandoned to get on the van, there wasn't a car in sight.

Kendall kissed Madame Buffet and said goodbye to Dudley and Georges. The pickup came into view and slid to the curb. "Here he is," Colby said. "I'll take your bag."

"Adieu, mes enfants. Don't let the bastards wear you down." Kendall grabbed Martine and kissed her, the reckless gray eyes moist with tears, and then kissed Colby. They threw two pillows and a folded blanket onto her shoulder. The arm she put up to hold them shielded the other side of her face. Colby grabbed up the suitcase and they went down the walk. He opened the rear door and she climbed in, not turning until she was hidden inside, seated on one of the bunks. He set the bag on the other. She smiled, while tears still overflowed her eyes. "Thanks, Trooper Colby. For this and that."

"Pas de quoi."

"Maybe sometime in another country."

136

"With luck. Goodbye, Champ." He closed the door, hit it once with his fist, and Roberto shoved it in gear. He watched it out of sight. Three blocks ahead it turned right, still alone. Nobody was following it.

He went back inside. Martine was on the phone at a stand on one side of the salon, and Madame Buffet and Georges were tidying up, carrying out the things they'd brought in from the van. Dudley had a bottle of whiskey and some glasses. He poured two jolts, handed one to Colby, and downed his with a gulp. He sputtered, and then, for the first time since he'd known him, Colby saw him smile.

"Wow! I needed that. All I can say is, you and Martine—oh, brother! It's finished!"

". . . not there! Oh, no!" Martine waved to Colby, her face enraptured, and returned to the phone. "Perfect. . . . But they've got Decaux? . . . And you've already called? Good. And thanks for everything." She hung up.

Colby had started to take his drink, but he put it down. He was too tired and too limp with reaction to swallow it. "Voivin?" he asked.

She nodded, with something like awe. "Colby, they ran out of gas in the Étoile, right in front of the east-bound lanes of the Champs Élysées——"

"Good God!"

"He says it's an absolute madhouse. The other man managed to sneak off and make it to the sidewalk, but two *agents* were bawling Decaux out for blocking traffic, and when he panicked and tried to run, they grabbed him. He started to put up a fight, so they really clobbered him. They may not realize yet the truck's on the stolen car list, but they will by the time they get him to the station and book him, and of course the tow-away crew will see the jumpered ignition switch. Voivin's already made an anonymous call to the *Police Judiciaire* and told 'em to look in that crate for one of the gang that killed Torreon." She sat down, the awed look still on her face. "You just wonder. Where will poor Decaux start, to find answers to all those questions?"

"You don't suppose he'll tell 'em what happened?" Dudley asked. "I mean, about this place——?"

"This place? Merriman, torture couldn't get it out of him. Don't you see, she might be still here, and the police'd find her. Or at least pick up her trail."

"All I can say is, you two. Oh, brother!" Dudley poured another drink and knocked it back. He did a couple of steps of a little jig. "And this afternoon I'll be on my way to New York!"

Colby had turned to the window again, just to savor the sheer joy of not seeing Decaux over there. At the same moment, a sleek but road-stained Ferrari swooped in to the curb with the grace of a diving falcon, and a leggy and vital-looking woman of about thirty-five with windblown dark hair bounced out of the driver's seat and came around in front of it before her escort could open his own door. She had on a suede car coat, and one end of the silk scarf about her throat was blown back over the shoulder of it with a sort of Dawn Patrol insouciance. He frowned. She seemed to be coming here. "Who's this?" he asked.

The man in the other seat was getting out now. He appeared to be about twenty, and could have just stepped out of a commercial for one of the more virile cigarettes, all wedge shoulders, flashing Latin eyes, and self-conscious masculinity. The woman laughed, brushed a playful hand through his hair, gestured toward the luggage in back, and came up the walk carrying a large manila folder. Her face was deeply tanned, giving her teeth that look of gleaming perfection of those of eighteen-year-old cannibals and aging screen and television personalities. Colby became aware that Dudley was standing beside him, making some kind of strangling noise. Behind him, Martine said, "No! Oh, no, it couldn't be!"

Sabine Manning came through the door, tossed the manila folder onto a table, and threw her arms wide. "Merriman! Aren't you glad to see me? Come kiss me."

Dudley, with the hue of a cadaver under fluorescent light, seemed unable to move but did make a croaking sound that could have been interpreted as a welcome. She kissed him and stepped back, still holding his arms. "Merriman, you look positively

138

ghastly. You should get out of this mausoleum and live a little. Cooped up in here with your slide rules and stock market reports making capital gains for me—you make me feel guilty. . . . And Martine, *darling*, how wonderful to see you again. . . . Carlito, sweet, just toss the bags there anywhere. . . ."

Carlito put the bags down and was soundly kissed and then programmed for the rest of the day while Colby was still trying to fight his way out of shock. ". . . go on to the Crillon—you can keep the car . . . and try to get a little rest, that is a long ride from Nice. I'll be busy all day with the publicity people, so don't bother to call me. Find out which *discothèque* is the one now, and pick me up here around nine. That's a dear, and bye for now. . . ."

Carlito departed. Sabine Manning turned to Colby. "I don't believe we've met."

"I'm sorry," Martine said. It was as near as Colby had ever seen her dazed by anything. "This is Lawrence Colby. Miss Manning."

"I'm so happy to meet you, Mr. Colby." She took his hand, held it warmly for a moment, and whirled to pick up the folder. "And it's so utterly sweet of you to meet me here. We won't have to lose a minute; we can get right to work on it——"

"But——"

"——first let me show you what I'm doing so you will understand why we have to give me a whole new image. You're familiar, of course, with the horrible sexy slush I used to write—I shudder when I think of it——"

Colby tried again to edge in a word, but saw Martine nodding and making frantic gestures behind her. She wanted him to accept the nomination for some reason, though he couldn't see why she insisted on prolonging the peril. Their only hope was flight. Miss Manning had the folder open now, and out onto the table cascaded a great pile of photographs, mostly eight-by-ten glossies, a size and type ideally suited for reproduction. She scattered and spread them. He had a blurred impression of sun-drenched seascapes and underwater scenes, the deck of a sailing yacht repeated over and over, barnacle-encrusted skeletons of ancient

139

wrecks, aqualungs, amphorae of every description, recovered arti-
facts, and people. It was on the people, strangely, that his attention suddenly came to focus, and he had just started back through
the photographs for a further study when he was caught up again
and swept along with the Manning vitality and enthusiasm. She
was addressing him.

". . . submarine archaeology. The invention of the aqualung,
Mr. Colby—or may I call you Lawrence?—has opened up a
whole new world of archaeological investigation. Try to imagine
it, five thousand years of the history of this cradle of civilization
just lying there covered by nothing but a shallow mantle of water,
waiting for the man with the aqualung to explore it. Merriman,
would you ask somebody to take the bags back to my room?
That's a dear. Biremes, triremes, galleys, ships of war, whole
cargoes of works of art lost on the way to Imperial Rome, and
who knows, maybe whole lost cities inundated before the dawn
of history——"

Colby noted that Martine was sorting through the photographs,
and he had an idea she was struck by the same curious aspect of
the yacht's personnel that had attracted his attention. Aside from
Sabine Manning herself, the entire membership of the expedition
seemed to consist of only slightly different versions of Carlito—
all Latin, sunburned, beautiful as Greek gods, of a median age
of nineteen, and—thanks to the scantiness of their swim trunks—
quite demonstrably and abundantly male.

There appeared to be eight or ten different ones, but then this
was a six-months' supply. No doubt the membership was fluid;
only the expedition went on as an established and continuous
entity.

He made another attempt to break in. "Yes, I know. I've read
quite a bit about it, and it's fascinating. But I'm not sure I understand why you want to change your image, just to do a book
about it——"

"Lawrence, I'm surprised at you. Of course I have to change it!
It's because this is so *vital*, so important, so fantastically wonderful, I want people to know about it—and nobody would believe
a word of it!" She threw her arms wide in a gesture of heroic

140

despair. " 'Oh, hell, it's just Sabine Manning—what does she know about anything but that dreary sex junk of hers?' They simply wouldn't believe I could write about something important, something that really mattered. . . . But I'd like to freshen up a little after that drive from Nice. Bring the photographs, Lawrence, and come on back to my room. We can go on with it while I'm having a bath; we haven't got a minute to lose. . . ." She had started to turn away when she saw the hesitant look on his face, and laughed. "Heavens, I mean through the door, dear boy. I don't expect you to scrub my back." She smiled at Martine. "Anglo-Saxons are so adorably shy."

"Yes," Martine said, with a smile he could have shaved with. "Aren't they?"

Sabine Manning disappeared into the corridor. As he gathered up the photographs and followed her, Martine leaned close and whispered, "I'm sorry. Just hang on, help should be here any minute."

She was apparently trying to buy time, but he was too confused and tired by now to figure out for what. After over forty-eight hours without sleep and living in a more or less continuous state of crisis, everything was beginning to blur and run together, Moffatt and Jean-Jacques and Gabrielle and Decaux and Sabine Manning all going around in a slow whirl in his head. He went through the study and into the white-carpeted bedroom. He heard water running into a tub, and Sabine Manning emerged from the bath. She smiled. "Please sit down," she said, indicating an armchair near the bed.

He sat down and put the photographs on a small table beside him. She threw off the car coat, tossing it and the scarf onto another chair, and opened one of her bags to take out a nylon dressing gown and some toilet articles, talking all the while.

"The whole trouble with Anglo-Saxons, or at least Americans, Lawrence, is our obsession with sex. Our lives are ruined by it, we're short-changed, we're robbed, mulcted, deprived, we're culturally and intellectually disinherited by this continuous stewing over something that's simply not that important at all—how old are you, dear?"

141

"Thirty," he said.

"Really? I wouldn't have thought you were anywhere near that. You're very attractive, you know."

She sat on the side of the bed, hiked the hem of the pale silk sheath halfway up her thighs, and began to unclip the tabs from her stockings. Her legs were as deeply tanned as her face, Colby noted, and very nice they were too. If this bombshell of vitality and hormonal fallout had ever really been the desiccated old maid he'd imagined and felt sorry for, no wonder Martine and Dudley had been stunned. As though she'd read his thoughts, she reached over to the night table, picked up a book, and tossed it to him. It was a copy of *These Tormented*.

"Take a look at that," she said, sliding her stockings down and tossing them aside. "The photograph on the jacket, I mean. There's the generic victim of this sex-preoccupation of ours, a woman not even half alive, shy, futile, plain, ineffectual, because she has no *interest* in anything, no curiosity, no desire for intellectual challenge, no capacity for total and utter absorption in anything—would you get this zipper for me, darling?"

She stepped over in front of him. He stood up and unzipped the dress. She turned, threw her arms wide, and cried out, "Look at me now! Look at my complexion, my eyes! I'm alive! I'm alive all over——"

"You are that," Colby agreed.

"——thrillingly, vibrantly alive right out to my fingertips. You see what archaeology has done for me? And why I have to tell people, make them *see*——"

She threw both arms around his neck and kissed him. He felt like a fly falling into a whirlpool of molten taffy, and tried to retreat, with about the same success. "Oh, I'm going to enjoy working with you, you dear boy. And I don't think you're thirty at all——"

They were suddenly interrupted by running footsteps and outcries from the salon. Colby ran out, and the sight that greeted him was enough to make him consider running back and throwing himself into the arena again with Sabine Manning, except that she had come out too. It was the end.

142

As well as he could piece it together afterward, with some help from Martine in regard to the cast, everybody must have landed at Orly at once. And now the wrath of Holton Press and the Thornhill Literary Agency descended on Dudley in the forms of Chadwick Holton, Senior, Ernest Thornhill, four attorneys complete with briefcases and forged and violated contracts, and one Parisian taxi driver shouting into the impervious and unheeding maelstrom of charge and countercharge and denunciation and denial that hell would freeze before he would take his pay in lire. In his mental state at the moment, Colby saw nothing unusual in the fact that the United States had abandoned the dollar; it was only afterward he remembered Thornhill had been in Rome.

There was nothing he could do, except pay the driver, who looked once more at the chaos in the salon and departed, shaking his head. "A madhouse."

"We are authors," Colby said with dignity. He lighted a cigarette and waited for the police to come and get him. Then he noticed that, strangely, Martine was completely unperturbed, merely watching and listening with interest. He went over to her.

She glanced at his lips. "Apparently Horatius, and the Alamo, are still on the record books."

He scrubbed at the lipstick. "These things just come over me, and I'm powerless. I once bit a lady cop in the subway in New York."

"Poor Lawrence. I'm sorry. I thought at thirty you'd be reasonably safe."

"She doesn't think I look that old. Do you know a good lawyer? Maybe if we called him right away——"

"Lawyer? Heavens, darling, the place is bulging with them now."

"I mean one of our own, to—you know—bring us cigarettes, and things like that."

"But Lawrence, don't you understand? We've won."

He looked over to where Sabine Manning was brandishing the manuscript over the cringing Dudley. ". . . you mean you intended to have this revolting piece of sexy slush published with my name on it?" she cried out as she threw it toward the ceiling. Sheets began to flutter down.

Colby shook his head. "We have?"

"Of course. It was just a case of hanging on till they got here. The whole thing's absurdly simple."

She walked out into the center of the salon and held up her hands. "Gentlemen, if I could have your attention for just a minute. . . ."

Some semblance of quiet had fallen over the room, and Colby had begun to sort people out. The white-haired man with the benign countenance who looked like Santa Claus was Chadwick Holton, while Ernest Thornhill was the austere type with the rimless glasses. The four attorneys were all young, equipped with narrow lapels and earnest expressions, and were more or less bunched at one end of the room as though drawn together by a shared distrust of the insanity with which ordinary people handled their affairs. Even Sabine Manning had broken off glaring at Dudley, and all eyes were on Martine.

"——If you are wondering why I'm interfering here," she went on, "it is simply because this entire fiasco is my fault. Having the novel ghost-written was my idea, not Mr. Dudley's. Which, of course, is the reason I called all of you yesterday and read you Miss Manning's telegram——"

Colby started.

"——Because I've wronged her, and I want to make restitution. I gather that in view of her new interests she has no intention of agreeing to publication of this novel—tentatively entitled *The Driven Flesh*—under her name."

"Not in a thousand years!" Sabine Manning cried out. Colby saw simultaneous shadows flit across the faces of Holton and Thornhill. They merely sighed, however. They had already heard Miss Manning's views on the subject, at some length.

Martine smiled. "I applaud Miss Manning's attitude. There is too much written sex already, and archaeology *can* be a lot more interesting, if properly approached. So, since in a way I have caused her money to be spent in having it written, the least I can

144

do to make amends is give the money back. Fortunately, I have a small income from a trust fund. I've already checked Mr. Dudley's records, and the sum involved is nineteen thousand dollars." She reached over on a table for her purse and took out her checkbook. "So if the assembled attorneys will draw up the papers for the transfer, I'll give her my check for the full amount and buy the novel from her. And perhaps Mr. Holton will publish it for me." She smiled at him.

Colby had given up trying to fathom it. He merely listened.

Holton returned her smile with a gallant little bow and one of his own. "I think we might. But since such honesty as yours demands honesty in return, I must warn you of the brutal facts of publishing life. Imitators of Sabine Manning are a glut on the market. A sale of three thousand copies would be about tops."

"But it's the same novel," Martine protested.

"The same novel, my dear young lady, but not the same thing. You could expect a return of—oh, say twelve hundred dollars. I'm sorry."

"Well——" Martine gestured fatalistically. It couldn't be helped. She still had to return the money.

"Well, I should hope so," Sabine Manning said indignantly.

In surprisingly few minutes, considering there were four lawyers involved, the papers were drawn up. It had been Colby's experience that even two attorneys trying to agree on the wording of something would have trouble ordering an extra quart of milk in much under half a day. Sabine Manning signed.

Martine smiled bravely as she passed over her check and took the bill of sale. "Incidentally," she asked, "what is the title of *your* book? I want to be sure to get a copy."

"*An Inquiry into Certain Analogous Practices in Afro/Roman Naval Architecture of the Second Century B.C.,*" Miss Manning replied proudly.

The collective shudder by Holton and Thornhill could have been felt in the next room, Colby thought. Martine pursed her lips and considered it. "Catchy, all right," she agreed. She turned to Chadwick Holton. "Should sell pretty well, don't you think?"

The latter's expression was that of a man watching himself

bleed to death from a severed artery. "With jacket endorsements by Moses and Julius Caesar," he said, "maybe three hundred copies."

"Oh, that is too bad." Martine turned to Sabine Manning. "I'm sorry."

"Why?" Sabine Manning shrugged. "I'm not writing it to make money."

Martine looked contrite. "Oh, I didn't explain, did I, why I suggested to Merriman that he have the novel ghosted?" Dudley cringed even lower, as though trying to disappear into his shoes. "Archaeological research seems to be so expensive, and with nearly all your money tied up in—shall we say, immature securities—"

The uproar broke out anew, with the attorneys once more in the thick of it. Amid cries of malfeasance, misfeasance, and nonfeasance, Dudley was denounced, fired, and threatened with an audit and prosecution. Martine held up her hand again for quiet.

"I think perhaps we're all being a little too heated about this. After all, the electronics stock *is* in Miss Manning's name, and will eventually come back. I'm sure that by retirement age, or maybe even by the time she's sixty, she will be able to resume her archaeological researches."

"*What?*" Sabine Manning's face was a study in sheer horror.

Martine appeared not to notice. She was frowning thoughtfully, and now she turned to Chadwick Holton. "There is one thing we've all overlooked, which might have saved the situation. I mean, Miss Manning doesn't want her name contaminated by any further association with sex novels, but she has *two* names—"

There was a gasp from all around the room.

Martine went on. "Would she have made any more money out of it, and been able to continue her archaeological studies, if she'd published both books? That is, *An Inquiry into Certain Analogous Practices in Afro/Roman Naval Architecture of the Second Century B.C.* under the name of Sabine Manning, and *This Driven Flesh* under her own name, Fleurelle Scudder?"

Chadwick Holton was regarding her with awe. "About fourteen

hundred dollars for both. Reverse the order, and you come out with a million two hundred thousand."

Martine looked blandly at Colby. "Maybe that's the way I should have put it."

As soon as the chorus of approval, including overwhelming endorsement by Sabine Manning, had died down a little, Martine held up her hand again. "But you're still overlooking something, gentlemen. Sabine Manning doesn't own the novel any more. I do."

In the ensuing and ghastly silence, Chadwick Holton asked, his face grave except for a suspicion of a twinkle in his eye, "How much?"

Martine considered for a moment. "Well, since I'm hoping to get away tonight for a vacation in Rhodes, I don't want to enter into any extended negotiations. So I think that for an offer of forty thousand from Miss Manning, plus a written guarantee that Mr. Dudley gets his job back, I'd sell right now."

They stayed at a hotel named for roses while being smothered in bougainvillea on an island that had been Zeus' gift to Helios, and ate their lunches on an awning-covered terrace with Moorish arches looking on the sea while an orchestra played Turkish-sounding music full of high woodwinds and the tinkling bells of camel caravans. They climbed on muleback to the Acropolis at Lindos and walked hand in hand through the old walled city where the cobbled streets that were as neat and unlittered as a floor had known the clanking tread of knights during the Crusades and sandal-footed Romans who followed the eagles a thousand years before.

They swam in the sea in the afternoons and afterward they made love and lay in bed under a fourteen-foot ceiling where wind banged the ancient shutters of their room, a flower-scented wind that somehow seemed to have a color, blue he thought it was. On the tenth day they were there they received an airmail letter from Kendall, posted in Gibraltar and forwarded by Martine's concierge in Paris. She had accepted Thornhill's offer to represent her as her agent in the production of future Sabine Manning novels.

They were lying on the beach in swim suits, drinking ouzo under an umbrella.

"And you knew all the time," Colby asked, "that if it came to a showdown you could apply the pressure?"

She shook her head. "Not till I saw those photographs. Before that it was a gamble. Calculated risk, rather. The telegram didn't sound like any embittered and heartbroken woman to me, with all that stuff about cocktail parties and press conferences. And Roberto's attitude didn't fit your theory either. I had an idea it was the other way."

"That he didn't leave her, she left him?"

"Sure. She wanted to broaden her horizons. And let's face it, poor old Roberto is pushing twenty-seven."

"Pretty creaky for that kind of duty, all right." He rolled over and studied her fondly. "You know, you're hell on wheels at pouring crème de menthe in watch movements."

"Incidentally, did you know this was a free port? And Swiss watches are just as cheap here as they are in Geneva——"

He put a hand over her mouth. "No you don't. Why don't we go up to the room?"

"What for?"

"Well, hell, do isometric exercises, tell elephant jokes, write postcards. There must be something you can do with a thirty-year-old fossil, with a reasonable amount of care."

She drew a fingertip along his cheek. "You may be right." They gathered up their gear and went in through the bar.

THE PERENNIAL LIBRARY MYSTERY SERIES

Delano Ames

CORPSE DIPLOMATIQUE	P 637, $2.84
FOR OLD CRIME'S SAKE	P 629, $2.84
MURDER, MAESTRO, PLEASE	P 630, $2.84
SHE SHALL HAVE MURDER	P 638, $2.84

E. C. Bentley

TRENT'S LAST CASE	P 440, $2.50
TRENT'S OWN CASE	P 516, $2.25

Gavin Black

A DRAGON FOR CHRISTMAS	P 473, $1.95
THE EYES AROUND ME	P 485, $1.95
YOU WANT TO DIE, JOHNNY?	P 472, $1.95

Nicholas Blake

THE CORPSE IN THE SNOWMAN	P 427, $1.95
THE DREADFUL HOLLOW	P 493, $1.95
END OF CHAPTER	P 397, $1.95
HEAD OF A TRAVELER	P 398, $2.25
MINUTE FOR MURDER	P 419, $1.95
THE MORNING AFTER DEATH	P 520, $1.95
A PENKNIFE IN MY HEART	P 521, $2.25
THE PRIVATE WOUND	P 531, $2.25
A QUESTION OF PROOF	P 494, $1.95
THE SAD VARIETY	P 495, $2.25
THERE'S TROUBLE BREWING	P 569, $3.37
THOU SHELL OF DEATH	P 428, $1.95
THE WIDOW'S CRUISE	P 399, $2.25
THE WORM OF DEATH	P 400, $2.25

John & Emery Bonett

A BANNER FOR PEGASUS   P 554, $2.40

DEAD LION   P 563, $2.40

Christianna Brand

GREEN FOR DANGER   P 551, $2.50

TOUR DE FORCE   P 572, $2.40

James Byrom

OR BE HE DEAD   P 585, $2.84

Henry Calvin

IT'S DIFFERENT ABROAD   P 640, $2.84

Marjorie Carleton

VANISHED   P 559, $2.40

George Harmon Coxe

MURDER WITH PICTURES   P 527, $2.25

Edmund Crispin

BURIED FOR PLEASURE   P 506, $2.50

Lionel Davidson

THE MENORAH MEN   P 592, $2.84

NIGHT OF WENCESLAS   P 595, $2.84

THE ROSE OF TIBET   P 593, $2.84

D. M. Devine

MY BROTHER'S KILLER   P 558, $2.40

Kenneth Fearing

THE BIG CLOCK   P 500, $1.95

Andrew Garve

THE ASHES OF LODA	P 430, $1.50
THE CUCKOO LINE AFFAIR	P 451, $1.95
A HERO FOR LEANDA	P 429, $1.50
MURDER THROUGH THE LOOKING GLASS	P 449, $1.95
NO TEARS FOR HILDA	P 441, $1.95
THE RIDDLE OF SAMSON	P 450, $1.95

Michael Gilbert

BLOOD AND JUDGMENT	P 446, $1.95
THE BODY OF A GIRL	P 459, $1.95
THE DANGER WITHIN	P 448, $1.95
FEAR TO TREAD	P 458, $1.95

Joe Gores

HAMMETT	P 631, $2.84

C. W. Grafton

BEYOND A REASONABLE DOUBT	P 519, $1.95
THE RAT BEGAN TO GNAW THE ROPE	P 639, $2.84

Edward Grierson

THE SECOND MAN	P 528, $2.25

Bruce Hamilton

TOO MUCH OF WATER	P 635, $2.84

Francis Iles

BEFORE THE FACT	P 517, $2.50
MALICE AFORETHOUGHT	P 532, $1.95

Michael Innes

THE CASE OF THE JOURNEYING BOY	P 632, $3.12
DEATH BY WATER	P 574, $2.40
HARE SITTING UP	P 590, $2.84
THE LONG FAREWELL	P 575, $2.40
THE MAN FROM THE SEA	P 591, $2.84
THE SECRET VANGUARD	P 584, $2.84
THE WEIGHT OF THE EVIDENCE	P 633, $2.84

Mary Kelly

THE SPOILT KILL	P 565, $2.40

Lange Lewis

THE BIRTHDAY MURDER	P 518, $1.95

Allan MacKinnon

HOUSE OF DARKNESS	P 582, $2.84

Arthur Maling

LUCKY DEVIL	P 482, $1.95
RIPOFF	P 483, $1.95
SCHROEDER'S GAME	P 484, $1.95

Austin Ripley

MINUTE MYSTERIES	P 387, $2.50

Thomas Sterling

THE EVIL OF THE DAY	P 529, $2.50

Julian Symons

THE BELTING INHERITANCE	P 468, $1.95
BLAND BEGINNING	P 469, $1.95
BOGUE'S FORTUNE	P 481, $1.95
THE BROKEN PENNY	P 480, $1.95
THE COLOR OF MURDER	P 461, $1.95

Dorothy Stockbridge Tillet
(John Stephen Strange)

THE MAN WHO KILLED FORTESCUE	P 536, $2.25

Simon Troy

THE ROAD TO RHUINE	P 583, $2.84
SWIFT TO ITS CLOSE	P 546, $2.40

Henry Wade

THE DUKE OF YORK'S STEPS	P 588, $2.84
A DYING FALL	P 543, $2.50
THE HANGING CAPTAIN	P 548, $2.50

Hillary Waugh

LAST SEEN WEARING . . .	P 552, $2.40
THE MISSING MAN	P 553, $2.40

Henry Kitchell Webster

WHO IS THE NEXT?	P 539, $2.25

Anna Mary Wells

MURDERER'S CHOICE	P 534, $2.50
A TALENT FOR MURDER	P 535, $2.25

Edward Young

THE FIFTH PASSENGER	P 544, $2.25

**If you enjoyed this book you'll want to know about
THE PERENNIAL LIBRARY MYSTERY SERIES**

Buy them at your local bookstore or use this coupon for ordering:

Qty	P number	Price
_____	_____	_____
_____	_____	_____
_____	_____	_____
_____	_____	_____
_____	_____	_____
_____	_____	_____
_____	_____	_____
_____	_____	_____
_____	_____	_____
_____	_____	_____
_____	_____	_____
_____	_____	_____
_____	_____	_____
	postage and handling charge	$1.00
	_____ book(s) @ $0.25	_____
	TOTAL	[ ]

Prices contained in this coupon are Harper & Row invoice prices only.
They are subject to change without notice, and in no way reflect the prices at
which these books may be sold by other suppliers.

**HARPER & ROW, Mail Order Dept. #PMS, 10 East 53rd St., New
York, N.Y. 10022.**
Please send me the books I have checked above. I am enclosing $_____
which includes a postage and handling charge of $1.00 for the first book and
25¢ for each additional book. Send check or money order. No cash or
C.O.D.s please

Name_____

Address_____

City_____ State_____ Zip_____
Please allow 4 weeks for delivery. USA only. This offer expires 4-30-84.
Please add applicable sales tax.